Reunion

Elizabeth Darin

Black Cat Books— Joliet, IL
ISBN: 978-0-578-97323-4
Library of Congress Control Number: 2021917830
Title: *Reunion*
Author: Elizabeth Darin
Digital distribution | 2021
Paperback | 2021

This is a work of fiction. The characters, names, incidents, places, and dialogue are products of the author's imagination, and are not to be construed as real.

For Mom
Check it out, I read a book.

Prologue
1992

I obviously don't remember this family reunion. There's proof I was there. I've seen the pictures of myself in the little handmade dresses and jumpers my mom's mom used to make for me sitting on the banister of the staircase and in the laps of my six to ten year old cousins, my grandfather, my grandmother, my very young looking parents…all of them took turns with the new baby. I can recognize some of the furniture in the house from those pictures…the same faded couch in the living room with the coffee table that I would later come to hate, but obviously had no strong opinions on in 1992. There were other things that were totally different of course. The old white appliances were still in the kitchen with the tile countertop which my grandmother was reportedly very pleased with at the time. Most of the bedrooms had wallpaper and a very strong 'lodge' feeling with heavy plaid comforters and pictures of moose and ducks. The rifles were proudly mounted above the fireplace, and there was one picture of nine month old me in a little brown dress and a headband with felt deer ears on it, surrounded by my cousins who were holding the rifles, a photo which brought glee to them year after year.

The reunions had been going on long before I joined in. Every Labor Day weekend, my grandparents had left Manhattan, driven across New York to a little town in the middle of nowhere on a lake. Back then, there were several houses that people used for summer homes or weekend getaways, and my grandfather had apparently purchased his piece of property for the hefty sum of $10,000. It was his gift to his wife Evelyn after his brand new company, Parker Marketing, hit it big. Over time, the small plots of land were bought up and now there were only a dozen or so houses scattered around the lake, mostly hidden by the trees, their large porches, docks, and second or third floor windows peeking through the foliage. The Parker family house was no different. The original house hadn't been more than a cottage, and there were a few black and white pictures of my very young grandparents in the late 50's or early 60's sitting outside the original one story house on a pair of rocking chairs, leaning against a '57 Chevy, and toasting with glasses of lemonade with people I never met. Back then, it was a reunion of friends. Grandpa George and Grandma Evelyn invited friends up to the little cottage for the long weekend, and as the friends got married and had children, the original house was torn down to make room for the expanding crew. Even though my grandparents had named the house 'The Cottage', there was no reasonable person who would call the eight bedroom, eight and a half bathroom house a cottage. My grandmother designed it specifically for multiple families to use, with certain rooms outfitted with a single king or queen sized bed and others strictly kid zones with two or even three sets of bunk beds. The inside stairs made quite the statement with large, dark wood banisters that flared out as the stairs widened onto the first floor. The living room and dining room were one large room with a huge wraparound porch overlooking the lake, with a staircase up to the second floor patio that lead to the bedrooms. Originally, the porches had been open, but they were later screened in, which I always imaged was a little sad since you no longer could look straight up from the second floor patio and see stars, but based on the average mosquito population, it was probably the most sensible thing to do.

The most interesting rooms of the house had to be the small third floor rooms. There were two small rooms with a full size bed in each room (the biggest mattress that could fit up the abnormally narrow staircase) and a jack and jill bathroom between them. The low ceilings and strange angles made shadows that made the room look like it had been painted six different colors, and the only way to get to them was the small staircase behind a door at the end of the hall. It always made me think it was a secret passage that only I knew about.

But that wasn't until years later.

Chapter One

Charlotte ducked down almost without thinking about it. She took the same route every day (weather permitting) to work and that low hanging branch was right at the end, about five minutes away from the library. She was probably going to need to change sides of the street soon, as she had to get lower every day and it was getting difficult to balance her bike and avoid getting smacked in the face by the branch. She wondered how far she could go without falling over? Every time she bent to avoid the branch, she felt like she was 6 inches from the ground, but every time she tried to do a cartwheel she thought she was doing a perfectly straight, Olympic quality turn with her legs perfectly straight in the air, a notion she lost after seeing a vidco of herself attempting one at Hannah's party last month, so what did she know. It was probably no more than a slight bow of the head to avoid a branch three feet above her head. She had no self-awareness on these things.

How does a person improve their sense of space? Is that something you can practice?

She got to the end of the sidewalk just as the light turned yellow (or she was 100 feet away from the end...who the hell knows) and stopped, using the opportunity to readjust her bag and grab her phone to check the time. She attempted to unlock her phone with the tip of her finger where the gray fingertips of her gloves were.

Smart phone gloves my ass.

She tugged the glove off with her teeth and unlocked the screen. How did she have eight emails? Who is emailing her this early?

7:36

Seriously. Why did she think it takes so long to get to work? She was always so early.

She'd been working at the library since she graduated, so just a little over 4 years. She'd been very lucky to get the position right out of college. Several of her friends (well, Facebook friends) were still living with their parents working temp jobs. Apparently, they were all suffering greatly as well, as her Facebook feed was nothing but her friends bemoaning their terrible lives. It made sense. Humans weren't meant to stay with their parents after the age of eighteen. At a certain point, someone is going to kill someone, no matter how much you all love each other. For her part, Charlotte had been lucky on one hand, and horribly unlucky on the other.

"What a horrible thing to say!"

That's what Hannah had said when Charlotte said she was lucky to have missed out on the personality problems that come with living with your mother in your late teen years. She was right. It was a terrible thing to have said, and it wasn't what she meant, at all. Of course Charlotte would have preferred to have arguments with her mother for years, rather than have attended her funeral at eight years old. She was just trying to be sympathetic to her friend and ended up saying something terrible instead. At that point, (how had she started college ten years ago already?) it had been ten years since the car accident, and Charlotte had just...adjusted to it. She wasn't happy with it of course, but it was just part of life. It was something to be dealt with and confronted. Now, eleven years after she had probably scarred Hannah for life with her caviler attitude, it was just part of who she was.

The one positive out of the situation (there she went again...finding the silver lining in death and carnage) was how her relationship with her father changed. Her dad, John Parker, had been a lawyer in his father's New York office. As the youngest of four brothers, all of whom worked for Parker Marketing, it was a big deal when he joined the staff. There were write ups in the paper, photo shoots, interviews with business magazines...it was all very exciting. Not for Charlotte and her mother, but it was exciting for the family, so Gwen Parker played the part of the dutiful wife, left her teaching job, and joined the Parker wives club, planning lunches and parties for important clients, wearing beautiful gowns at art galleries and the theater, and all kinds of other frivolous functions that somehow rule the upper classes. Charlotte remembered the apartment they lived in with the high ceilings and wall of windows that she always found a little frightening. They were kept so clean, she sometimes thought the windows had been removed and she was going to fall the twenty-some stories to the street. She remembered Claudette, the nanny who spoke French to her and rode with her in the big black town car to and from school, and flying in spall, private planes to small private islands.

Looking back, it was the kind of life most people probably fantasize about. Charlotte looked back at it with distain. Poor little rich girl. Such a hard life. Boo fucking hoo.

But her biggest memory from the New York days were of being lonely. Claudette was nice, but she never hugged her or played games. She rode in the big black town car to and from dance classes, school, swim lessons, and for walks in the park, and always brought her in to see her parents before bed. She remembered sitting on her canopy bed as it got dark out with a semi-circle of stuffed animals looking at her and telling them all about her day or setting up long domino paths and knocking them down in interesting patterns or running her own fashion shows with scarves and hats stolen from her mother's closet and carefully returned so no one realized they'd been borrowed.

That all changed in the summer of 2000.

Charlotte yawned, waking her up enough for her to notice the light had changed. She shook her head slightly and double checked all the traffic had stopped. By all the traffic of course, that meant the completely empty intersection. Not one car had gone by the entire time she had been stopped. It wasn't that no one lived in town, but most everyone commuted to Burlington, so by the time Charlotte left for work, most of the city 9-5ers had already left. Charlotte's dad did have an office in Burlington, but he preferred the small town life and did most of his work out of the city. He had three or four partners that ran the show in the city, and it meant he only had to check in once or twice a month. The rest of his time was spent taking care of the mundane legal aspects of small town folk. He had a reputation for his honesty and relaxed nature with people. He always explained things in plain language since 'most people don't and don't want to speak lawyer' as he often said, so people liked him. He also did way more pro bono work than he probably should, but still managed to make sure Charlotte had everything she needed growing up.

John Parker left his office in Manhattan the day he got the phone call from the hospital that his wife had been in an accident and never went back. His brothers had his office cleared out and sent everything to him months later. Maybe they figured he just needed time and would come back to work eventually. Maybe they figured he sold the penthouse apartment in Manhattan because he just wanted to get a different place or a brownstone that hadn't been he and his wife's home. Maybe they thought the three bedroom, two bathroom ranch style house in a quiet Vermont neighborhood was some kind of vacation home. Maybe they were just lazy and had to wait for someone to mention the now vacant corner office in the legal department. Really, it was probably a little of all those things, plus the shock that someone would walk away from that life.

Charlotte's phone rang. She coasted into the library parking lot and up on the sidewalk where the bike parking was, swinging her bag around her body so she could reach her phone. She swiped her thumb across the screen to answer it, only to be foiled again by the damn gloves. She pulled it off and swiped again.

"Hey Dad." He was the only person who ever called her, especially this early. Anyone else would have texted.

"Hi Charlie. You on your way to work?"

"Just got here. What's up?"

"They shut down Broadway," her father said matter of factly.

"Really?"

"Yeah. I really thought this COVID thing would be under control by now, but I was talking to Matthew yesterday and he said they have to refund his season tickets because everything just shut down."

Charlotte shared her father's surprise. It was the top story in every newspaper and almost always came up in every conversation. It was one of those surreal things that no one really paid any attention to a month ago, but now was all anyone could talk about. She wondered if this was how the Spanish flu pandemic started a hundred years earlier.

Charlotte shook it off.

"I'm sure it'll just be a few weeks dad. I can't imagine it's going to go much farther than that."

"You're right. It's just weird to see it."

"Is that why you called Dad? Giving me the latest COVID news?"

"That, and I wanted to double check the time for your thing tonight."

Charlotte rolled her eyes.

"Art show Dad."

"I know," he said with a smile in his voice.

"You know I wrote it on your calendar last time I was over, right?"

"Did you?"

Charlotte could hear him get up from what she assumed was the kitchen table where he had most likely been reading the paper and finishing his second cup of coffee. She figured she had a good 15 seconds while he shuffled over to the wall calendar she bought him (a new one every year for Christmas) then another 45 while he figured out what day it was. She put her phone on speaker and set it down on top of the trash can while she grabbed her bike lock and threaded the blue plastic coated chain through her front tire and secured it to the bike rack.

"There it is. 6 til 9. You want me to bring you some dinner?"

"Yeah, that'd be great. You want to come at like, 5? We can eat and you can help me finish set up?"

"Sure. Always happy to be slave labor."

"So nice to have you at my beck and call," she laughed as she took her phone off speaker and brought her phone back up to her ear, choosing to ignore the fact that her phone had just been on a garbage can...maybe she had some disinfecting wipes in her office.

"Your wish is my command Charlie. Mexican or sushi?"

"You hate sushi. You obviously want Mexican and guac is delicious, so it's a date."

He laughed.

"You know me so well. See you at 5."

"K. Bye Dad."

"Love you."

"Love you too."

Charlotte hung up and slipped her phone back in her bag, grabbing her keys in the same motion. She unlocked the door and let herself in, then turned around and locked it behind her. She shivered a bit as she adjusted to the warmth inside. It wasn't horribly cold out…in fact it was relatively warm for mid-March...but she was starting to regret riding her bike today. It was going to be way colder after the show. Oh well. She could thaw herself out with a hot bath if she needed to.

Her shoes squeaked a little as she strode through the quiet hallway into the main part of the library. She turned right at the desk and switched keys to her office key, opening it and hanging her bag on the coat rack in the corner. She hit the start button on her little 4 cup coffee maker (having filled it the night before...a little habit she picked up after one too many mornings where she started the machine with no water in the tank or no coffee in the filter...or both) and hit the start button on her computer. While coffee was brewing and the computer was booting up, she hung up her coat, then checked the drop box to gather the day's papers. She plopped the papers on the desk for Janice to set out, and then returned to her office, grabbing her mug and walking over to the small kitchen next door. She grabbed an ice cube from the tray, dropped it in the cup, and then poured a little flavored creamer on the cube before returning to her office, just as the coffee maker had made about one cup's worth of coffee. She filled her cup and sat down at her desk to check her email.

It was a comfortable routine. She always liked knowing just what was going to happen and had things down to a fine art in her little world. Life could be unpredictable, but not here. Not in her little world.

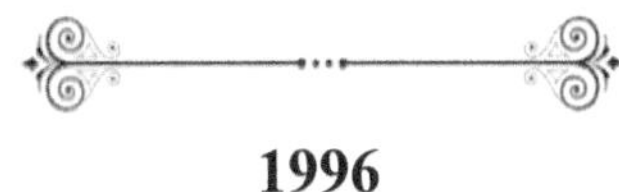

1996

Today was Thursday.

Dance class is on Thursday. Why wasn't she at dance class?

Where was Claudette? Claudette always takes her to dance class on Thursday. This wasn't the way to dance class. The way to dance class had tall buildings and lots of people. This wasn't the right way.

Charlotte sat on her knees and watched the trees go by out the window. She rested her chin on her crossed arms, but the stretch was uncomfortable. She started to stand up on the seat.

"Charlotte sit down," her mother gently scolded as she tapped her butt. Charlotte turned around and flopped down, looking around the big, rectangle car. Her dad was sitting on the seat across from her, reading some papers from the open briefcase next to him and her mother was sitting next to her, reading a book. She looked down on the floor and saw Bun Bun, his floppy ears sprawled out on the black carpet. She scooted off the seat and walked over to pick him up, but barely got two steps before her mother was tugging on her arm.

"Sit down!" She looked across to her husband. "I told you we should've taken the town car. I'd really prefer her in a car seat."

"I can have the car pick us up," he said without looking up.

Charlotte wriggled, trying to get free.

"Bun Bun!!" she cried, the panic of a four year old separated from her beloved stuffed bunny erupting in what was becoming a dramatic display.

"John."

Without looking up from his papers, John Parker uncrossed his legs and used his right foot to push Bun Bun safely into his owner's arms. Charlotte scooped him up and hugged him tight, the panic of the last 30 seconds quickly forgotten as she climbed back on the seat next to her mother.

"Where we going?"

"Where ARE we going," her mother quietly corrected.

"Where ARRR we going?"

"Honey I told you. We are going to Grandma and Grandpa's house on the lake. Remember? You get to see all your cousins."

"Who my cousins?" Charlotte asked, not having the slighted idea what 'cousin' meant.

"Who ARE my cousins."

Charlotte huffed. "Who ARRRRR my cousins?"

"Well, there's George..."

"That Grandpa!" Charlotte laughed at her silly mother's mistake.

"Yes, honey. Grandpa's name is George, but you also have a cousin named George. He's 14, so he might not want to play with you. That's a pretty big kid."

"I'm big!"

"Yes you are, but George and his sister Elizabeth are 14 and 13, so they are REALLY big kids."

"Like giants?" Charlotte said with wide eyes.

Her mother smiled. "Not that big."

"Ok good. That too big," Charlotte said, feeling much better.

"Then," her mother continued, "there's Charles and William. They're twins, which means they were born at the same time and have the same birthday."

"Wow!"

"I know! They're 12, so again, kinda big. Then there's Travis, who's 11, and his little brother Trevor who's 10. They are kinda...rough boys, so you might not want to play with them so you don't get hurt."

"They aren't that bad Gwen," Charlotte's dad chimed in.

"Were you there last year? It was like living in the monkey house."

"Gwen…"

"No, I take it back...monkeys are better behaved."

He put the paper he was reading down and took off his glasses. Charlotte braced herself for angry daddy. He huffed loudly, then his face broke and he laughed.

"Fair point. I'm surprised we didn't find them flinging shit at each other."

"What's 'finning shit'?"

"A very naughty word that we don't say honey," her mother said, trying not to laugh.

The ride started getting bumpy and Charlotte stretched her neck to see what was happening. Her father folded his glasses and tucked them into his suit jacket pocket and closed his briefcase. He smiled at Charlotte. "Here we are Charlie."

The big brown and green house appeared out of the woods like a castle from a fairy tale. The large windows reflected the trees, making it hard to tell where the house ended and the woods began. Beyond the house, the sun was gently setting over the still lake, broken only occasionally with the call of a bird or a fish breaking the surface of the water. The big car turned slightly to the left, parking next to two other big, black cars. The trunks of the other cars were open, and there was a flurry of activity as the drivers pulled bags out and walked them up the stairs to the wide porch leading to the large wooden double doors. Charlotte watched them go back and forth as the car rolled to a stop. She heard the engine stop and a moment later, the door opened. Charlotte let her father help her out and she looked around. She knew this place...she remembered it from a long time ago...Grandma gave her cookies.

"Hello John! Hello Gwen!"

Grandma Evelyn stood in the doorway, a calm figure among the luggage flying past her from the cars. She wore a cream colored pants suit, tailored perfectly to her petite frame. Her gray hair was pulled back in a tight bun, out of the way of her large gold earrings.

"And where's my little princess?" she said, bending down slightly and smiling, pretending not to notice Charlotte holding her mother's hand.

"Grandma!" Charlotte yelled as she ran up the stairs and hugged her tight.

"Be careful baby! You don't want to break Grandma."

"I'm a tough old bird John. I don't think a three year old is going to break me," she said with a smile.

"I'm four!" Charlotte said, pulling back from her grandmother and defiantly putting her fists on her hips.

"You are!" Evelyn said in mock surprise. "Well then, I suppose I'll have to give you four cookies!"

"Yeah!"

Evelyn turned and entered the house, holding Charlotte's hand, her heels clicking on the wood floor and echoing up through the large open cabin. Charlotte looked up to the top of the windows. She thought the windows at home were big, but these were enormous, reaching all the way to the roof line of the three story home and following the peak to form large triangles that looked out onto clouds. Below the triangle windows, large windows and sliding doors opened onto a screened in porch, and Charlotte could see rocking chairs and a hammock, with a matching porch on the first floor right below. Ahead of her and to her left, Charlotte saw a huge staircase...she sat on that railing before...why did she sit on that railing?

Her grandma lead her around the corner to the right and Charlotte saw a huge table with more chairs than she could count which were blocking a big plate of

"COOKIES!"

Charlotte ran up to the table and reached toward the plate. Grandma pulled the plate toward her.

"Now, you get four cookies because you're a big four year old. You count them out for me."

Charlotte carefully laid out the cookies on the table as she counted to four.

"Hey Mom. Can I show you something?"

Evelyn patted Charlotte on the head and stepped away as Charlotte finished counting to four. She then carefully picked up the cookies one by one, trying to carry all four and struggling to figure out how to do it as she heard the stampede coming across the floor. She looked up just in time to see Travis and Trevor running toward her.

"Sweet! Cookies!" Travis said as he grabbed four off the plate with one hand and another five with the other. He shoved one handful in the pocket of his shirt and refilled the empty hand with another five cookies.

"Hey buttmunch! There's only three left for me!" Trevor yelled as he pushed his brother and grabbed the last three cookies off the plate.

"She's got some," Travis said, spitting pieces of cookie as he spoke, then turning towards the back porch and running for the door.

Trevor looked down at Charlotte, who was standing still through this whole display, still clutching two cookies in each hand. Trevor dropped his three cookies in his shirt pocket, then reached out and emptied Charlotte's hands in one motion. Charlotte jumped back in shock and looked at her empty hands then back at her cousin, who laughed, popped a cookie in his mouth, and ran after his brother to the back porch.

Charlotte's eyes started to water.

Today was Thursday.

She should be at dance class.

No one took cookies away from her at dance class.

Chapter Two

Charlotte smiled as she handed the books back to Sophie. She came in every two weeks like clockwork to check out a new romance book. She grabbed a flyer for tonight's art show.

"Hope to see you back in an hour or so Sophie."

Sophie smiled and left. She probably wouldn't be back. What if no one came? What if she did all this planning and no one bothered to show up? Charlotte watched Sophie as she left and felt her chest clench up. It spread to her throat and she tried to slow her breathing to no avail. Why did she let herself get so worked up over this shit? She pushed the chair back and stood up. A walk around the library usually calmed her down. She could go over everything for the show. That would give her something to do. She stepped out from behind the desk and started a brisk walk around the shelves.

It was slow today...weirdly slow for a Friday. Usually there were more people picking up weekend reading, weekend movies...fuck...was this going to be the show tonight? Totally dead? Her throat tightened up again. She glanced down at one of the book return carts. There were five. She quickly picked them up and started putting them away. A task. Something to focus on.

She had chosen the date very carefully. It was mid-March, so spring break was just starting for the local school district, but the college had had break a few weeks earlier, and midterm projects were due, so she had offered to show the art student's work. Some of them were really good, and the students seemed really excited about it. Maybe they didn't realize it wasn't a real art show. Then again, it was a show for art. People were going to be able to purchase pieces. There was a bar. That made it legit, right?

Charlotte put the last of the five books away and started toward the back conference room. The majority of the pieces were already up and she started around, going over in her head which pieces were going to head out into the library and which ones were going to stay back here. She found herself in the back corner, looking at her own pieces. Maybe it was self-indulgent to give herself the back corner. Maybe she should put her own pieces out in the library.

No, the sculptures will make the pathway back to the paintings. The lighting in here is better for paintings.

She had considered it for weeks and she knew she had the best layout. It was just last minute jitters. She was just freaking out over the potential lack of people.

Maybe fewer people would be better. People could really take time looking at pieces. If it was too crowded, people would get frustrated and leave.

There...sweet justification for failure. She felt so much better.

Charlotte finished her walk through of the conference room and circled back to the circulation desk. Janice hung up the phone just as Charlotte approached and looked up.

"Hey. That was the bar service guy. He said they are running a few minutes behind but will be here in plenty of time to start serving at 6."

"Ok thanks. He's the one I'm really concerned with."

"Oh no worries Char," Janice said with a glint in her eye. "If that guy had stood you up, I would set up my own stash faster than I can drink myself under the table."

Charlotte laughed and thanked her before heading back into her office. Janice was awesome. She was brash, and funny, and constantly made Charlotte do things she was uncomfortable with. They'd met in undergrad when Janice was briefly in the history department with Charlotte. Janice had bounced around to several majors in school, but somehow managed to finally get an English Literature degree. Charlotte had managed to get both her Bachelor's and Master's degrees in the time it took Janice to finish her Bachelor's, but Janice had certainly had more fun and experiences along the way. At one point, she had taken a semester off and went to Japan. Charlotte still wasn't sure how she managed to survive...she didn't speak Japanese and actually hated Japanese food, but somehow, she survived and came home with some great stories, after she missed a connecting flight in Hawaii and ended up living on some vegan organic farm commune for six weeks. Charlotte couldn't live like that. She had her day scheduled to the minute. She knew how many paperclips were in her top desk drawer. Her clothes were organized by season and color in her closet. Janice, on the other hand, walked into her house, right into her perfectly organized closet, grabbed the first four outfits she saw, threw them in a bag, and kidnapped Charlotte to Vegas for a weekend for no reason other than she was bored and wanted to see how Charlotte would react to Thunder from Down Under.

Janice had started at the library three years ago. Charlotte knew it wasn't exactly the most ethical hire she had ever made, but Janice did have a literature degree, so it didn't really matter that Charlotte had offered her the job after Janice had shown up late one night, drunk off her ass because her parents had kicked her out and she didn't have a job or anywhere to go. Janice had done great since then. As flighty as she could be, she really did know her stuff, and actually started leading the library's book club and spearheading a lot of new ideas for the summer reading program. Plus she was funny as fuck.

"So...time to start talking birthday plans."

Charlotte looked up and saw Janice hanging on her office door frame with a wicked grin on her face. Charlotte furrowed her brow.

"Who's birthday?"

"Yours you twat," Janice said as she scooted into the office and flopped down on the grey couch along the wall.

Charlotte leaned back in her chair and looked at Janice.

"What are you talking about? It's March. My birthday isn't until November."

"Yes, so we need to get planning! Where are we going?"

"I'm going to get back to work. We have an art show to get ready for," Charlotte said as she glanced at the clock. Her dad would be there with dinner in about 15 minutes, then she needed to change...

"No no no," Janice said as she sat up and leaned in towards her looking dead serious. "You are turning 30. We need to go big."

"You're turning 30 in January. I'm turning 29. Why don't you focus on your own birthday?"

"Because I have a husband who has to plan the party and make it amazing, so I'm covered. As your best friend and work wife, it is my sworn duty to make your 30th birthday one you will not remember due to alcohol poisoning."

"Again, 29th birthday. And what's the point of making it so special if I'm just going to black out?"

"You'll have the police report to remember it."

Charlotte laughed and rolled her eyes.

"Ok, I'll leave that in your capable hands. In the meantime, I think I see some of the art students here to help you set up the show."

Janice looked over her shoulder at the half dozen college students standing at the desk then back at Charlotte, who was already holding out the set up diagram she was about to ask for. Janice snatched it and stood up calling back over her shoulder.

"It'll be one for books Char. Your mug shot will be epic!"

Charlotte rolled her eyes but inwardly was already looking forward to it. She didn't really want to do anything crazy, but maybe a fun trip...a cruise or an all-inclusive resort. Whatever Janice planned, Charlotte was convinced it would be way more fun than anything she could have come up with. Janice and her husband Matt threw the most epic parties and took trips all the time. Matt worked for some travel company and got all kinds of free trips. He really was the perfect match for Janice…they both loved travel and dropping everything to take off to some club or new restaurant in New York. Once, Janice called in to take the day off because they had jumped on a plane the day before. They literally went to the airport and asked the agent where they could go for $500 or less and ended up in Michigan for two days. Sometimes Charlotte was really...*really*...jealous of the life they lead. It all just seemed so exciting. Of course, the practical side of her had no fucking idea how they did it. Obviously, Janice didn't make a whole lot of money working at the library, and Matt was making money, but Charlotte couldn't imagine it was really that much. At one point, Janice had said something about how they paid everything on their credit card and got the miles so they always flew for free, but she couldn't image they really made enough for all the trips they took. Maybe most of the trips were paid for by Matt's work.

Of course, Charlotte knew she was not one to talk about other people's finances. She wasn't some poor, struggling post grad like most of her friends. While her father had walked away from the high paid Manhattan life he started in, he wasn't hurting. From the outside, John Parker blended right into his suburban neighborhood. His house was average, and frankly, a little dated. He drove a four year old car. He took one or two trips a year, and they were never anything super extravagant. Last year, it had been a Caribbean cruise that he treated Charlotte to. They shared a basic stateroom and didn't really splurge on any drink packages or shore excursions. With his official severance package from the company and several investments he had, John Parker had paid cash for his little suburban house, and when Charlotte had graduated from grad school, her graduation present had been her own little house a few miles away from his house. This was information she kept to herself. So many of her friends were still living with their parents or renting teeny tiny apartments together, it seemed cruel to tell them she owned a house outright at 26. She refused to ask her father for anything else though and was saving up to do a big remodel on the kitchen. Any time she felt like it was taking forever to save up the $40,000 she wanted to really do it right, she immediately felt guilty thinking about how lucky she was that that was the kind of thing she could choose to spend her money on, rather than praying she was just going to make it to the next paycheck. She owed a lot to her father. He was always taking care of her.

"Hey Charlie."

And just like that, there he was, guacamole and a burrito in hand. Yet more taking care of his little girl.

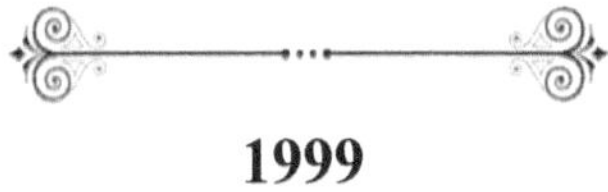

1999

Charlotte watched the clouds move silently from one window to the other. It was so neat how the big ones could be in more than one window at once, and the small ones moved from triangle to triangle. She tried to keep track of which cloud was which, but they kept changing shape as they changed from one window to the other. She repositioned her head on the pillow on the big brown couch, craning a little as she looked up the two stories to the windows on the top floor of the cabin. It was quiet in the house. No one had been inside when they got there, so her mother had told her to stay on the couch while she and her father brought things up to their room and got settled. Last year, they had taken her out of school on Friday so they could come up on Thursday night, but Charlotte had begged them to let her stay in school Friday. They were having Fun Friday and got to have double gym and recess, plus she was star student for the week, which meant she got to be the head of the line all week...she didn't want to miss all that! So now it was getting dark on Friday afternoon, and they were in the house by themselves. It was nice. It was usually really loud in the house, and Charlotte didn't get to sit on the couch. Her cousins usually gave her a pillow and she sat on the floor when everyone was in the living room. It was nice to spread out on the couch.

"Well Charlie, I just got off the phone with Uncle Mark."

Charlotte turned around and looked at her father as he came down the stairs, pushing a button on his phone and slipping it back in his jacket pocket.

"Everyone went out for dinner, so how about a PB&J?"

"Yeah!"

Charlotte excitedly jumped off the couch and ran over to the dining room table while her father started opening cabinets. Charlotte watched her mother come down the stairs and look at her father with a little smirk.

"John...what are you up to?"

"Trying to feed our child," he said as he closed another cabinet and stepped back with his fist on his hip. "Mom and Dad's driver usually stocks the kitchen, but I can't find anything."

Gwen smiled and softly guided her husband out of the kitchen. "I'll take care of it." She effortlessly pulled a plate down and opened a second cabinet, retrieving the peanut butter that had hidden so well a moment ago. John headed over to the table in the next room and pulled his laptop computer out.

"John. Really? You brought that thing?" Gwen scolded as she spread the peanut butter.

"I have some work to get done. It'll be a solid 45 minutes until everyone gets back from dinner, so I figure I can get it done now."

Gwen pulled the jelly out of the fridge. "I thought this was going to be a work free weekend. We stayed in town an extra day so you could get everything done."

"It's only a little bit. Shouldn't take more than an hour. I can probably get it done before everybody gets back." With that, he started typing away.

Gwen sighed quietly and put the plate in front of Charlotte. She happily scooped it up and took a bite as Gwen stroked her hair.

"Sweetie, do you want to do some drawings for everyone after you eat?"

"Yeah!" Charlotte exclaimed through a mouthful of peanut butter.

There was a new art teacher at Charlotte's school this year, and she had really taken off in class. The new teacher wore really pretty clothes and had these great scarves that she always had wrapped up in neat ways. She also let the students wear smocks and get really dirty with paint which Charlotte loved. The art teacher from last year was fine, but Charlotte really liked Miss Nelson. She'd already gotten two positive notes home from her about what a great artist she was, and Miss Nelson said if she worked hard, she could be the second grade representative in the winter art show.

Gwen came back to the table with one of the bags she had packed and put it on the table. She reached in and pulled out a set of markers and an oversized drawing pad. Charlotte's eyes widened and she quickly ate the rest of her sandwich.

"What do you want to draw for everyone?"

"I'll do family portraits."

Miss Nelson was teaching them how to draw people and families, so she wanted to practice. Then she'd be good enough to be in the art show. Her mom helped her figure out who went with who:

Grandpa George and Grandma Evelyn

Uncle Matthew with the black hair and Aunt Margaret who always wore the big necklaces. Cousins George and Elizabeth who had the same blonde hair as their mother.

Uncle Mark and Aunt Julia who always wore the tight skirts on her small frame and spent lots of time on the phone. Cousins Charles and William who Charlotte carefully drew to look the same since they were identical twins.

Uncle Luke who Charlotte drew with the cigarette in his mouth and Aunt Ana who always looked sad, and Cousins Travis and Trevor, who she drew in action with lines behind them since they never stopped moving.

Charlotte was just putting the finishing touches on Travis and Trevor as she heard the door open. Aunt Julia came in first, her handbag hanging on her elbow and her heels clicking on the floor. Her phone was up to her ear and Charlotte heard little phrases…"cutting out"… "I'll have to get that next week"… "my assistant has that information" as she walked through to the back porch and closed the door behind her. Uncle Matthew was close behind her, with Aunt Margaret on his arm. They were talking softly to each other and immediately brightened when they saw Charlotte's dad get up from his computer to give them a big hug. Travis and Trevor blew past the group hug and ran up the stairs, pounding the entire way up before slamming their bedroom door behind them. Uncle Luke stopped in the doorway, taking one final drag off his cigarette before tossing it off the porch and entering the house, making a beeline for the kitchen where he helped himself to a beer. Aunt Ana followed him, taking his coat as took it off and hanging it in the hall closet. Charlotte heard her mother sigh quietly as she bent over to pick up the bottle cap from his beer after he tossed it in the general direction of the trash can.

Finally, Grandma Evelyn entered. She took a step inside and turned to watch her husband climb the stairs with Uncle Mark following a step behind him.

Grandpa George was an imposing figure, even at 79 years old and walking with a cane, he managed to stop any room he entered and totally own it. Standing over six feet tall, with a strong physique and strands of black still mixed with his grey hair and goatee, he walked slowly but firmly into the house, taking a moment to survey the house. He smiled slightly as he saw all four of his boys together, beaming in his own sense of accomplishment. John separated himself from the group and received a firm hand shake and hug from his father before getting the same from his older brother Mark. Grandpa George strode across the living room to his favorite chair and landed with a less than graceful flop that he somehow managed to still make dignified.

Charlotte collected her drawings and ran over to her grandfather.

"Grandpa! Look! I made you a drawing!"

Grandma Evelyn came over and stepped behind her husband as he took a small pair of glasses out of his jacket pocket and rested them on his nose. He took the paper out of Charlotte's excitedly shaking hand.

"Well that's just lovely Charlotte," he said with a big smile as he handed it back to her. Grandma Evelyn intercepted.

"I'll go put this in my bag sweetie."

Charlotte beamed and turned back to the rest of her relatives who were all talking over each other and hugging. She took a few steps towards everyone and tried to remember who everyone was. Even though they all lived in the city, she didn't see her cousins very often, and they all looked like grown-ups, so Charlotte had a hard time telling them apart. She looked out on the porch and saw Uncle Luke lighting a cigarette. She knew who he was because he was the only grown up she knew that smoked. A small blonde lady stepped out to him and handed him a can of beer. Charlotte looked down at her drawings. Aunt Ana. Standing near the fireplace was Aunt Margaret...she recognized her big necklace...talking to her dad while keeping one hand on the young man standing next to her. Charlotte walked towards them.

"...and then he starts at Harvard next year."

"Already accepted?" Charlotte's father asked.

"It helps to drop a few names." Aunt Margaret winked and turned towards Charlotte.

"Hello Charlotte. How are you?"

Charlotte held up the picture she drew of Aunt Margaret, Uncle Matthew, George and Elizabeth. Aunt Margaret daintily took it from Charlotte and smiled.

"Oh well isn't that lovely. Thank you dear."

She stood back up and continued talking to Charlotte's dad. Charlotte tried to follow, but it didn't make any sense. She looked at her cousin George. He looked like an adult in a tidy polo shirt and khaki pants, but his mom kept saying words like 'classes' and 'study' so did that mean he was a kid?

Charlotte shrugged and saw Aunt Julia pacing on the porch, holding her new cellular phone to her ear. She pulled up the drawing of Uncle Mark, Aunt Julia, and the twins and headed out to the porch. She started pulling open the door to present her drawing to Aunt Julia when she heard quick steps behind her and then felt a hand pushing the slightly opened door close.

"Whoa there Charlotte," Uncle Mark said as he quietly pushed the door closed. "Aunt Julia is on the phone, so let's leave her alone for a little bit."

"I just wanted to give her my drawing," Charlotte said.

"Oh that's awesome," he said as he took the drawing, glancing at it briefly while he looked out the glass porch door at his wife and guided Charlotte in the opposite direction. "I'm going to go put it in my room ok? Why don't you go show that picture to Grandma and Grandpa?"

Charlotte took a few steps away and turned back to Uncle Mark, who started his own pacing by the door. She turned back to her drawing of Uncle Luke, Aunt Ana, Travis and Trevor and wondered if she should show it to Grandma and Grandpa. She started back over toward them but stopped as she passed the coffee table. There was something there that hadn't been there a minute ago. She took a few steps closer and picked it up...a folded piece of paper. She put down her drawing and started unfolding the paper. As she opened the last fold, her heart sank. Staring back at her were the smiling faces of Uncle Matthew, Aunt Margaret, William, and Elizabeth, the happy family now cut in half with the creases in the paper. All her time and care...now a crumpled mess on the coffee table. She felt her eyes strain against the tears welling up, her throat felt tight. She turned quickly and ran for the stairs, running up as fast as her little legs would carry her.

"Charlotte."

She froze, having only made it up half the first flight of stairs, and turned back to see her grandmother at the bottom looking up at her.

"I wanted to tell you again how nice that drawing is. Your mother was just telling me how well you are doing in art class and I imagine you're the best artist at school."

Charlotte smiled and the tears dried up instantly. She took a few steps down towards her grandmother.

"You really like it?"

"Absolutely. And I should know," her grandmother smiled as she took Charlotte's hand. "I wouldn't be on the Met's board of directors if I didn't know a thing or two about good art."

The two of them took a seat on the stairs and Charlotte leaned into her grandmother as she squeezed her. Charlotte inhaled deeply, the familiar perfume wafting through the air and surrounding her.

"You can tell a great deal about a person by their taste in art," her grandma started. "Someone who can see the true beauty of a work of art can see beauty in so many places. I think you can see the beauty in things Charlotte. Keep capturing it."

Charlotte smiled and hugged her Grandmother tight.

She'd have to make her more drawings this weekend.

Chapter Three

Charlotte threw another mint in her mouth after yet another rancid, bean scented burp. She caught a glimpse of herself in the mirror, trying to suck in her gut and failing miserably. She could have passed for someone in their first trimester the way that burrito was sitting in her. She said a little prayer that her control top pantyhose were made of some kind of magic that could contain her food baby and headed back out into the library.

It was going really well. So far, Janice had counted about 150 people come through and there were more trickling in. Charlotte finally felt like she could relax a little. She had decided that if 50 people came, it was a success, and with more than 70 still in the library and people coming in and out, she was confidently calling it a success. A big part of her wanted to celebrate with a glass of wine, but food baby told her she should think twice about that one.

Charlotte walked slowly past the sculpture pathway, watching the college students and other local artists talking to people about their work. A few of the sculptures were marked as 'sold' so Charlotte smiled. A few college students probably sold their first art piece today. She really hoped that encouraged them to keep creating. Painting was just a silly hobby for her. She knew she was never going to make a career of it, and really didn't want to. Not a very stable career. She liked knowing exactly how much she was bringing home every month and not being dependent on someone else's opinion of her work. Although she did get a little thrill from the idea of selling a painting. She'd sold a few here and there... $50 here, $100 there...nothing major. Her dad had one she tried to give him for Christmas but he insisted on buying it from her, so she told him it would cost him $1. He paid the dollar in pennies.

She made her way back to the conference room. There were about 15 people milling around, sipping wine and talking to artists. She looked back in the corner at her own display and to her amazement, there was a man staring at one of her pieces. She stepped up behind him, careful to keep her distance so she didn't startle him or break him out of his quiet contemplation.

She started contemplating him. She hadn't expected anyone to really look at her paintings, but he seemed mesmerized. He was about her age, maybe a little older, as she could see a few lines forming at the corner of his eyes. He was a little taller than her, which meant he was probably a good 5 inches taller than her when she wasn't wearing her ridiculous heels she only wore with her little black dress. He was wearing nice, fitted jeans that cupped a tight little ass she couldn't help staring at as it poked out under his suit jacket and a polo shirt that looked like it was custom made for him. His black hair was a little longer than she thought it should be for a guy his age, but it was so nicely styled, it was hard to think it was wrong. She couldn't help staring, and was very glad he seemed preoccupied with the painting because she would be so embarrassed if

Food baby strikes again.

Charlotte caught the rancid, bean burp before it escaped, but not before it made a lovely little half hiccup, half growl noise that was just enough to pull her mystery art fan out of his trance. She quickly cleared her throat and tried to pass the food baby's revenge off as a cough.

He was looking at her. No, there had to be someone else. She turned slightly, expecting to see someone else. No one. She looked back at him, suddenly very aware of the silence.

Shit...say something!!

"Are you enjoying the art show?"

"Yes. Such a cool idea," he answered, taking a step toward her. "I was getting coffee in town today and saw the flier in the coffee shop, so I had to stop by."

"Oh, are you an art professor? Collector?"

"Just an admirer," he laughed at himself a little. "I won't say I actually know anything about art."

"Do you know what you like? You don't have to know anything formal about art to appreciate it. If you like it, then its art."

He looked at her. Charlotte froze. He was really looking *AT* her. Like he had been looking at her painting a second ago. She wasn't sure what to do. Men didn't generally stare at Charlotte, and normally, she didn't like anyone looking at her, but this was different. It wasn't weird, or threatening, or uncomfortable. He was just, really seeing her.

"That's a really good point." He extended his hand. "Peter Li"

She took his hand and shook. "Charlotte Parker. I'm the head librarian."

"So this was your idea?"

"Yes. I dabble in painting, so I suppose it was a little selfish way I had to show off some of my own work, but I like giving the college kids a place to display their work, and there are a few other local artists we have that are pretty good."

"I'd love to see your pieces Charlotte Parker." He took a step back, presumably so she could lead him on.

"Actually these are mine." She gestured to the paintings he had been looking at a minute ago. She smiled and drooped her head a little. "I suppose it's too late to get your honest opinion on them now."

"Oh no, I'm a very honest guy," he said with a mischievous smile as he took a step toward her. "I would never falsely inflate your ego." He turned and stepped next to her, turning back to the paintings. "I was looking at this one, the one with the triangles and the clouds inside. I really like the juxtaposition of the sharp angles with the clouds. It's like two things that don't go together, but they make perfect sense in the painting."

Charlotte watched him while he spoke. He glanced back at her after he finished and his cheeks flushed a little. Charlotte felt her own cheeks flush. Damn he was cute.

"So I either sound like I know what I'm talking about or I sound like a real jackass."

"I was impressed with your use of 'juxtaposition'. Very arty."

Arty? What kind of idiot says 'arty'?.

"Well thank you. I try to insert big words into my everyday language. And, I would like to buy this piece, Charlotte Parker. How much are you asking?"

Charlotte smiled. She didn't think she'd sell anything. She hadn't even priced any of the paintings.

"What are you thinking?" she asked, trying to sound confident when really she was just so taken aback by the whole thing she had completely blanked.

He looked back at the painting and crossed his arms. After a beat he looked back at her.

"$500."

"Five..." Food baby strikes again. By a small miracle, she caught the bean belch in her throat, saving her a world of embarrassment. She silently thanked the food baby for giving her a second to process what had just happened. She swallowed and looked at the painting, trying to be cool, collected herself, and turned back to him.

"Sold."

"Fantastic," he said as his phone started buzzing in his back pocket. He took it out and read the screen, then put it back in his pocket as he turned back to her.

"This is probably way out of line, but I need to head out. I saw that people are supposed to come back tomorrow to pick up purchases, but I may or may not be in town. Is there any way you could have this delivered to my mom's house? I may or may not be there, depends on some work stuff I might be taking care of."

"It's not a problem. Just give me the address."

"Fantastic, thank you."

He followed her to the circulation desk and she grabbed a post it for him. He jotted down an address then reached in his jacket pocket and pulled out a checkbook. He filled it out and handed it to Charlotte.

"Thank you very much, Charlotte Parker."

She watched him as he walked out then looked down at the check. Yes, it really was for $500. That had happened. She smiled and grabbed a 'sold' sticker before heading back to her painting. Someone really liked her work!

Chapter Four

*A*rrived.

Charlotte's phone reverted back to the larger map and she parked in front of the two story house on the corner. It was sweet, with a wrap around porch and black shutters, nice bushes and a weeping willow out front.

Or maybe this was the house she would die in.

She hadn't really thought about it until she was driving that morning...she didn't know that guy. Maybe there was a sweet old lady in this house and Peter Li (if that was his real name) had bought the painting for her. Maybe he was a serial killer and she was going to be locked in the basement in ten minutes.

She texted Janice. She had it worked out that she'd text every ten minutes as a check in, so she let Janice know she'd arrived, then opened her door and stepped out of her car.

FUCK!

Her feet hurt so much. She normally didn't wear those heels when she was doing so much walking, but she hadn't expected to be on her feet as long as she had been the night before. She closed the door behind her and hobbled over to the back door to retrieve the painting from her back seat. She pulled it out, closed the door, and looked at the sidewalk up to the house. It looked twenty miles long. Standing still wasn't too bad, but she knew she couldn't just stand there. The sooner she delivered this thing, the sooner she could go home. She was planning on doing some grocery shopping after this, but all she wanted to do was go home and put her swollen, angry feet up. She had no food in the house, but that's what delivery was for. She could get a pizza and just eat it all day while binge watching The Office and not moving. The sooner she forced herself up that damn sidewalk, the sooner she could shove pizza in her mouth.

She winced audibly as she started forward. Each step made her want to hack her own feet off. Maybe this guy was a serial killer and he'd cut her feet off. She might thank him.

She made it up the three steps to the porch and rang the doorbell. After a few beats, the door opened and a small Asian woman appeared.

"Well hello! You must be Charlotte. Come in!"

She opened the door and stepped back inside, calling up the stairs.

"Peter! Charlotte is here with the painting!" She turned back to Charlotte. "Peter told me all about the art show. I don't know why he didn't bring me, but I think he was just excited to buy me something. He loves to surprise me." She closed the door and stepped back. "So let me see!"

Charlotte held the painting up and Mrs. Li smiled.

"Peter was right. This is very nice. You are very talented."

"Thank you," Charlotte said as she heard a door close upstairs. She looked up and saw Peter come down the stairs. He was wearing fleece pajama bottoms and a t-shirt that managed to hug his arms in the perfect place. His hair was a bit disheveled and fell in his eyes as he yawned and blinked rapidly as if he had just gotten up.

"Charlotte Parker," he said as he hit the bottom of the stairs and held out his hand. Her cheeks flushed. He was very well put together last night, and he was obviously not put together this morning, but somehow, he was even better looking today than he was last night. She took his hand and shook it.

"Good morning. I didn't think I'd see you this morning."

"Yeah I ended up on a conference call at 1am so it was just easier to stay here."

"A conference call at 1am?"

"Yeah I know. I have some business with some people in England and it was just easier to schedule a meeting on their time. It was nice enough that they were willing to talk on Saturday so I had some recovery time." He turned to his mother.

"You like the painting mom?"

"Oh yes. You do know how to pick the nicest pieces for me."

"Good. Let's hang it up."

"Oh no! No holes in my wall!"

"Mom, relax. I'm going to use the hook that sticks to the wall."

He took off down the hall with his mother in tow.

Charlotte smiled. It was cute to see how other people related to their parents. In a way, it was the same for everyone. Parents never really saw their kids as adults.

"Would you mind bringing that in here?"

Mrs. Li motioned for Charlotte to come down the hall. Charlotte took a step and the smile immediately disappeared. Her fucking feet! When she got home she was burning those damn shoes. She hobbled her way down the hallway into the room at the end of the hall. Peter was standing on the couch, pressing a command hook on the wall. He held it there as he turned to she Charlotte wince her way into the room.

"Are you alright?"

"Yeah," Charlotte lied.

"Really? Because you don't look alright."

Charlotte rolled her eyes and came clean.

"My feet are killing me. I usually don't wear those heels I was wearing last night for long periods of time, and they were really not made for standing and walking for hours on end."

"Sounds like you need a better pair of shoes," he said as he stepped down off the couch. He smiled and took the painting out of Charlotte's hands. His hand grazed hers a little as she handed the painting over. Dear God he was good looking. He looked her up and down. She instinctively sucked in her stomach a little.

"What are you, about a seven?"

Seven? Like on a scale of one to ten? She'd always thought of herself of more of a four, four and a half...

Shoes! Fuck! He meant shoes!

"Um…yes. Seven wide actually. I have a hard time finding wide width dress shoes."

Oh my god stop talking about shoes!!

He nodded a little and stepped back up on the couch, bringing the painting up and hanging it, taking a second to straighten it out before stepping backwards off the couch.

Mrs. Li clapped her hands.

"It looks wonderful! Thank you Peter." She gave him a hug and turned to Charlotte.

"It's just lovely. You are a real talent!"

Charlotte blushed. "Thank you ma'am."

The three of them stood there silently. Mrs. Li and her son looked back and forth at each other as Charlotte stood awkwardly in the room. Should she leave? Yes, she should, but she felt weird just hobbling off, and the thought of moving again was not a pleasant one. Mrs. Li widened her eyes and tilted her head toward Charlotte. Peter suddenly seemed to understand.

"Thank you mom." He turned toward Charlotte. "Let me walk you out."

He kept a nice slow pace with her as they continued down the hallway.

"Again, thank you so much for bringing the painting here. If I'd known I was going to be in town, I would've come and gotten it myself."

"It was no trouble," Charlotte half lied. Obviously it was some trouble getting up on a Saturday and being a delivery girl while she bled internally from the feet, but in the greater scheme of things, it really wasn't that big of a deal.

They reached the door and Peter stepped in front of her to open it. He looked at her again...really looked at her. She stood and tried to look anywhere but him, but her eyes kept coming up and meeting his. They were deep, brown and calm...thoughtful and seemed to reach all the way into her soul. She knew she probably looked like a love sick teenager, but she didn't care anymore. She just wanted to keep looking at him. It felt like a perfect, electric moment. She never wanted it to end. But it did. Quietly, as Peter unlatched the door.

"It was really nice to meet you, Charlotte Parker."

"It was nice to meet you too, Peter Li."

She hobbled out of the house, trying her best to walk normally and failing miserably on what at this point had to be broken stubs where feet once were. She flopped down in her car with a grateful sigh as she felt the blood rush through her foot stumps. It was going to be so nice to put what was left of her feet up when she got home. She pulled out her phone and shot Janice a quick 'I'm not dead' text while she enjoyed a few minutes of foot freedom before she had to use her right foot to drive home. She looked back at the house. She smiled as she thought about Peter. God he was cute. Not that there was anything to be done about it. Someone as gorgeous as Peter probably had a different girlfriend every night. Besides, it's not like she would have the courage to do anything like ask him out. Girls like her didn't go out with guys like him. Girls like her didn't ask men out. Girls like her didn't go out period. She started the car and gave the house one last glance. Girls like her didn't go out with great looking guys, but at least he would give her some fun fantasies to keep her company on the couch today.

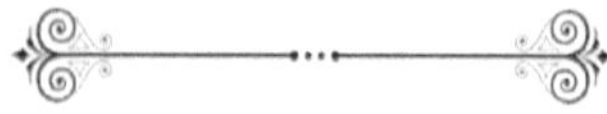

Charlotte hadn't just stayed on the couch all day Saturday, she stayed there all day Sunday too. At about 3 in the afternoon Sunday, as Season 9 of 'The Office' was wrapping up on Netflix, she finally took the 'Are you still watching' prompt as a sign that maybe she should peel herself off the couch and take a shower. She'd earned a weekend off she told herself. The art show had been a huge success, with about half the display pieces being sold, another couple donated to the University, two being donated to the library, and a few people signing up to be on the library donor list. She might need to make this an annual event. Of course, when she thought about the amount of work that she put into the show, she thought weekly root canals might be more fun.

She should have gone grocery shopping over the weekend, but around 7 on Saturday, she realized Monday was her late day, so she could get it done before she went in at 1 on Monday. She also took the opportunity to treat herself to take out for lunch, something she always felt guilty about after buying groceries, but it was always kind of fun to have that sandwich waiting for her in the fridge at work. Not exactly the most financially responsible thing to do, but little treats didn't do too much damage to her budget...as long as it wasn't too often.

At 12:30, Charlotte strode in the front door of the library, her bag of fast food glory in hand. Janice looked up and smiled at her.

"Hey boss! Three more people signed up to be on the donor list today because of the art show. One lump sum and the other two are monthly gifts!"

Charlotte beamed. Generally speaking, her library was doing alright financially. They were pretty well supported by the community, but she knew that could always go away. They were always going to need private donations as well and giving money to the library wasn't always a sexy way for people to donate money, so she was grateful for every dollar.

Charlotte stepped into her office and plopped her food down on her desk. She turned to hang her coat up and saw Janice standing in her doorway with a package.

"This came for you this morning," Janice said with a mischievous glint in her eye.

"Ok. Why are you looking at me like that?"

"I'm very interested in the mystery package."

"I get packages all the time."

"No, the library gets packages all the time. This is hand addressed to you," she explained as she came in, put the box down on her desk and sat on the small couch against the wall. "Open it!"

"Ok. This really isn't that exciting."

Charlotte opened the package and revealed a green and black shoebox. She opened the lid and pulled out a sleek, black dress shoe. It had about a two inch heel, a rounded toe, and rubber soles, with a cushy gel interior. Size...7 wide.

Janice picked up the box and looked at the other shoe.

"Holy shit Char. These are Thunderbolts."

"What?"

"Thunderbolt. It's that fashion company in New York that makes the 'practical fashion' line."

"What?" Charlotte was genuinely confused. She hated clothes shopping and fashion really wasn't on her radar. Janice on the other hand, was an encyclopedia of all things fashionable and trendy.

Janice rolled her eyes.

"Super expensive, super trendy, super sexy shoes. Who the hell sent these to you and can I be friends with them?"

Charlotte looked at the return address on the packaging. It was an address from New York City she assumed was the office address. Then she saw the note taped to the lid of the shoebox, labeled 'My favorite artist.' She pulled the note off the lid and opened it, reading it out loud for her very excited audience.

Charlotte,

I was hoping to take you out for dinner next time I'm in town, but was worried you'd wear those uncomfortable shoes again. I'd hate to have you in pain just to have dinner with a fan of yours. Give me a call if you're interested.

Peter

Janice smacked Charlotte's arm, harder than Charlotte was ready for.

"Holy shitting Christ Char!! No one gets asked out like this! This is like, Sandra Bullock, Julia Roberts romantic comedy level shit!"

Charlotte was beaming but was trying to keep her idiot grin concealed. Janice was right...people didn't get asked out like this. At least, average looking nobodies like her didn't get asked out like this. Maybe good looking people got asked out like this. Charlotte didn't get asked out like this.

Reality finally smacked Charlotte in the face.

"Janice, he's not asking me out."

Janice held up the shoe and cocked her head.

"Seriously!" Charlotte exclaimed. "He bought one of my paintings for his mom. I brought it over to her house. I helped him hang it in her living room. He's probably just looking at thanking me for the help."

Janice tossed the shoe back in the box and sat back.

"You cannot be this dense. This isn't a thank you dinner. This is a 'I wanna get in your pants' dinner."

"No one is getting into anyone's pants Janice," Charlotte said reasonably as she put the shoe she had been holding back in the box and replaced the lid.

"Ok, but you're calling him, right?"

Charlotte exhaled and sat back. She knew Janice wasn't going to let this go, but Charlotte couldn't imagine someone as good looking as Peter was interested in her. This had to be just a thank you. Although, he didn't have to reach out to her. It was a business transaction, nothing more. He bought a painting, she delivered it. That should be the end of it. Then again, why would he have reached out if he wasn't interested?

No. Charlotte shook of the delusional fantasy and put the shoes away. Guys like that didn't go out with girls like her.

2000

The rain collected in the corner of the window, hung on for a few seconds, then blew away. Then it collected again, hung on, and blew away. Over and over.

Charlotte watched it. Over and over. Her seatbelt cradled her face as her eyes watched the rain on the window. Over and over. How many times had she watched it? She should've been keeping count.

The car bounced over a pothole and she hit her head on the window, knocking her out of her water induced trance. She hated the new car. When they were in the big car, it felt like they were ice skating across the road. Or sailing on a ship across calm water. In this car, she could feel every single rock on the road. She readjusted herself, wincing as she pulled her thigh off the hot, sticky, plasticky seat. She hated the seats in the new car. She pulled her knees up to keep her legs from sticking again below her shorts.

She looked up at her dad in the driver's seat. He had one hand on the steering wheel, the other elbow on the door frame propping his head up. They'd ridden in silence together ever since Vermont. He'd picked her up from school early (pulled her right at the beginning of gym) and they headed out. She hadn't really wanted to speak to him the whole time. She knew he was taking her out of school early today and she wasn't going to be in school tomorrow, but tomorrow was Friday, which meant she was going to miss art class. The third grade classes only had art on Wednesdays and Fridays. It wasn't like her school last year where she had private art lessons every day. She only got art two times a week, and he was making her miss one of them!

Mrs. Randolph was the only thing she liked about her new school. Whenever she heard the art cart coming down the hallway, she perked up immediately. At her old school, the art room had high ceilings with lights that Miss Nelson could change the brightness of. There was a kiln that the older kids got to use and shelves of student made pottery. Mrs. Randolph had a cart with paint or markers that she wheeled in to Charlotte's classroom every Wednesday and Friday. Just a cart. But every time that squeaky cart came in the room, Charlotte imagined she was back in the art room at the old school. It wasn't hard to do. Mrs. Randolph managed to transform her cart into a beautiful, light, airy art room with nothing more than some paint, markers, or glue sticks. Charlotte loved Wednesdays and Fridays.

Her dad inhaled loudly and turned the car to the right onto the familiar driveway in the woods. Charlotte perked up and looked out the window. The rain wasn't pounding the car as hard anymore as they entered the woods, and Charlotte could finally see the trees and lake clearly through the raindrops. Her dad pulled the car in line to the left next to the two limos and a big black town car. He turned the engine off and sat back in his seat, exhaling thoughtfully. They sat in silence for a moment as the raindrops got fainter, John staring somewhat blankly out the window, Charlotte looking at her father. He was wearing the same green polo shirt he wore all the time now. Maybe he had a bunch of them and they were all the same. Charlotte hadn't checked his closet. Not that the clothes would be in the closet. Most of her dad's clothes were still in boxes on the floor of the big bedroom in the new house. She was still getting used to seeing her dad in polo shirts, khaki pants, and jeans. He never used to wear those kinds of clothes. He only used to wear suits. She hadn't seen him in a suit since the funeral.

He broke out of his trance and turned to Charlotte. A slight smile crossed his lips, but his eyes were still sad.

"I know it's been a really rough month Charlie," he started, his voice catching a bit. Charlotte was still getting used to her father's new voice. It was slower and quieter, without the confident edge it used to have.

"A really rough month," he continued. "And I just want you to know how proud I am of you. You've adjusted so well to everything..." he trailed off and looked up at the cottage.

"I think this is what we need," he said, a little of his old confidence returning. "Some time with family."

He turned fully towards Charlotte.

"Family is the most important thing Charlie. Life is going to pull you a thousand different ways. Things are going to seem really important in the moment, but don't let that get in the way of family. Family first and always Charlie. Do you understand?"

Charlotte shook her head. She didn't really, but it seemed like he really needed her to agree with him. Her dad smiled, tears gathering in his eyes. He reached into the back seat and squeezed Charlotte's hand, then turned back around, wiped his eyes, and got out of the car. Charlotte unbuckled her seatbelt and opened her door. She swung her feet out and stopped herself right before she dropped down into the puddle that had formed right outside her door. She pushed herself off the door frame and hopped over the puddle, then joined her dad at the trunk. Two of her grandparent's staff were coming down the stairs of the house as John pulled his and Charlotte's bags out of the back. They quickly whisked the bags away from him and were jogging up the stairs as Grandma Evelyn appeared at the door.

"John. Charlotte."

She opened her arms and Charlotte and her father were practically pulled in with a gravitational force. The three of them embraced and Charlotte felt like hiding for the rest of the weekend inside her grandmother's knee length sweater. The last time she'd seen her grandmother was at the funeral. Her dress had had a black fur collar that Charlotte had rested her head on the entire service. Charlotte ended up with a red mark on her arm where her grandmother had hugged her for almost the entire day. She was sad when the mark went away.

Evelyn released them but let her hands linger a bit before ushering them in the doors. Her heels clicked on the floor as the three of them entered the living room. Charlotte could hear laughter and conversations which came to a sudden stop as John, Evelyn, and Charlotte entered the room. Uncle Matthew and Uncle Mark each took a sip of their drinks almost in unison. Aunt Margaret sat forward on the couch while Charles, William, George and

Elizabeth looked at each other nervously before looking back at the trio that just entered and putting their cards down on the table. Aunt Ana quietly took a step forward and rested her hands on the sofa. Out on the porch, Uncle Luke took a long drag of his cigarette and put it out on the pillar before tossing it into the bushes. Charlotte couldn't see Aunt Julia. She was probably up in her room working or taking a phone call.

Charlotte had never heard the cottage so quiet. More strange to her though was how everyone was looking at her. She couldn't remember ever having this many sets of eyes on her, especially here. She shifted nervously toward her father, scooting a step behind him in what seemed like slow motion. Everyone just stared at them.

Grandma Evelyn's heels cracked through the silence.

"George dear," she called out to the younger George who quickly snapped his head towards his grandmother.

"Why don't you light a fire. Lindsey brought marshmallows for the weekend. I think it would be fun for you little ones to make s'mores."

Charlotte's cousins all looked at each other. They knew when Grandma said 'little ones', she meant her grandchildren, but Charlotte was really the only little one left. Trevor was closest to Charlotte and he was 14. Charlotte had watched him roll his eyes at the suggestion of s'mores. Lindsey, Grandma's cook, was already coming out the kitchen with a tray of graham crackers, chocolate bars, and marshmallows and headed toward the back door.

"Elizabeth, get the door for Lindsey. George, there are matches and fire starters in the shed by the fire pit. I think the skewers are in there as well, on the shelf with the outdoor pots and pans. If not, I'm sure Lindsey knows where they are."

She clapped her hands sharply twice, then beamed her million dollar smile that seemed to light up the entire room.

"Off you go little ones! Its stopped raining, so it's a lovely evening for a fire and some cousin time without us grown-ups."

She shooed everyone towards the door. Charlotte heard a slight grunt to her left and turned to see Travis begrudgingly lift himself out of his chair and walk towards the door, shoving Trevor slightly to get him moving as well. Aunt Margaret whispered something to Elizabeth who nodded and ran upstairs, presumably to fetch something. Charles and William headed out, casually mentioning to George they'd gather some twigs. Elizabeth returned from upstairs with a small bag and approached Charlotte with a soft smile. She held out her hand to Charlotte. Charlotte instinctively stepped back and grabbed her father's hand, looking up at him.

"Go on Charlie. It'll be fun," he said with a strain.

Charlotte looked from her father to her grandmother, who both looked at her with sad smiles. Why was everyone pretending to be happy? She looked over at her cousin Elizabeth who had the same sad, strained smile. Charlotte took a step out from behind her father and took Elizabeth's hand, and the two of them slowly headed out door.

The fire pit was close to the lake and to call it a 'pit' was an understatement. There was a full pavilion with outdoor seating for what Grandma Evelyn called the 'Rustic Kitchen'. The shed was the size of a standard two car garage and had an entire kitchen's worth of plates, silverware, and cookware, cushions for the chairs, three canoes, a paddleboat, and a pair of jet skis. To the side of the pavilion, there was a standard fire circle with stumps as seats. As Elizabeth and Charlotte arrived to the circle, Lindsey was quickly returning from the garage with a pile of cushions for the stumps. As she put cushions down, Charlotte's cousins took seats. George and William appeared from the woods with arms full of twigs and dropped them near the fire pit.

George and William started piling wood and Lindsey brought them matches and fire starter. Charlotte adjusted herself uncomfortably on the stump as Elizabeth brought the little bag to her.

"Here Charlotte. My mom saw this and wanted you to have it for the weekend."

Charlotte took the bag and quietly thanked her as she opened the bag. Inside was a little brown teddy bear. She pulled it out and looked at it, seeing her own reflection in the bear's sad, bead eyes. She glanced up, feeling like more than just the bear was looking at her, and saw all her cousins staring at her. What was supposed to happen now? Was this some kind of magic bear? Did it do something Charlotte was unaware of? She darted her gaze slowly back and forth between all her cousins, and they all just stared back at her, looking like they were waiting for something transformative. After what seems like an eternity, Charlotte quietly tucked the bear in her elbow and hugged it close to her body. The young adults in the circle seemed to exhale in unison as the awkward moment passed and the business of fire building and s'more making continued.

Charlotte listened without really comprehending as her cousins laughed and talked about things she really wasn't interested in. At one point, Lindsey gave her a s'more, having made it for her and she took a few bites before quietly tossing the rest of it in the fire. She yawned at some point and suddenly realized it had gotten dark. She quietly got up and saw Elizabeth turn toward her looking concerned.

"I'm just tired," Charlotte said quietly and Elizabeth nodded, watching Charlotte head back to the house.

Charlotte quietly opened the back door and slipped inside. Grandpa and Grandma had gone to bed...Charlotte could see the light on under their closed door. Her father was nowhere to be seen...probably up in their loft room already. Uncle Luke was sitting on the big easy chair drinking something and listening to something while Aunt Ana sat quietly nearby. Uncle Matthew, Uncle Mark, Aunt Margaret and Aunt Julia all sat in the living room quietly chatting. Charlotte quietly walked to the stairs and started up to her and her father's room but was only about halfway up when she heard her name and stopped. She looked through the slats of the stairway handrail, ready to ask what they wanted, but stopped herself short when she realized they hadn't seen her, they were just talking about her. She sat on the step and leaned in a bit.

"She can't possibly be happy. He took her away from everything. Do you honestly think she's getting French lessons and ballet in that God forsaken town he's in?"

"I'm sure he'll come back soon," Uncle Matthew said calmly to his wife. Aunt Margaret just shook her head. Apparently this was not the first time they had had the conversation.

Aunt Julia put her wine glass down and looked at Margaret.

"I just hope he comes back soon. You know that Jennifer and Robert Howard are getting divorced?"

"They're going through with it?" Margaret perked up. "I thought they had just decided to keep pretending."

"No, Jennifer finally pulled the plug. Robert's last affair got pregnant and Jennifer finally said she'd had it. It'll take some time for all the dust to settle of course, but I want John back in town. Jennifer would be perfect for him."

Mark looked at his wife.

"Julia, the man's wife *just* died. I think he needs a little more time before you try to marry him off."

"Obviously. But the whole thing should time out. Her divorce is probably going to be a little messy and it's going to take a few months. Maybe a year or so if it gets really nasty. By then, John should be ready."

Margaret chimed in.

"They would be good together."

"Exactly," said Julia, taking another sip of her wine. "Jennifer and John always got along, she's well connected, she's well bred...they just make sense."

"It would be good for John to be with someone more suited to our lifestyle. Gwen tried but she never really fit in," Mark agreed with Julia.

"My point exactly."

"It's still a little early to be talking about this," said Matthew. "We still need to get him to come home."

"I give it until Christmas," said Mark. "He'll miss the family at Christmas and move back. We'll be able to keep selling the idea that he took an extended leave of absence for another month or so, then we can say he's been working on out of state contracts until he comes back. Fresh start in the new year."

"God I hope its earlier than that," Margaret said as she put her wine glass down. "Ugh," She sighed in disgust. "This God awful coffee table."

"You can't replace it Margaret," chided her husband.

"I know," she sighed. "I just hate the fact that we are now stuck with this monstrosity just because Gwen bought it. It's not like an oil painting. The value doesn't increase when the artist dies."

Charlotte backed up on the stair and leaned her back against the wall.

She was suddenly very glad for the teddy bear as she hugged it tighter.

Chapter 5

"**D**id you call him yet?"

Janice wrapped her scarf around her neck and glared at Charlotte. She'd asked the same question every twenty minutes for the last four hours.

Charlotte sighed and put another book back on the shelf.

"No, because unlike some people, I've been working all day," she jokingly reprimanded Janice.

"I worked today!" Janice haughtily claimed, matching Charlotte's mocking tone. "I researched my next trip and decided Matt and I are headed to Argentina!"

"Well you have been busy. Do you need tomorrow off?" Charlotte teased.

"No, I think I have time to recover. However, I can't leave to start my recovery until you call him."

Charlotte admitted defeat.

"Fine. I promise I will call him. Go home."

"Not until you call him."

"I'm busy! I promise I will call when I get back to the office. I have his number in the shoebox."

"Call him now," Janice said with a devilish smile as she produced the note Peter had taped to the top of the shoebox. Charlotte sighed heavily and realized she was not going to get out of this. She pulled her phone out of her back pocket and took the number.

Janice watched her dial and hit send...she was taking her sworn duty to her friend very seriously.

"This is Peter."

"Hi Peter, this is Charlotte."

"Charlotte Parker. Hello," Peter said in a softer tone.

"I just wanted to call and thank you for the shoes. They are lovely."

"And shouldn't make you limp after a night of wear, so there's an added bonus."

"Definitely a plus," she agreed. She glanced up at Janice who's eyes were getting wider with every word. Charlotte needed to move this along.

"So anyway, I just called to thank you for the shoes, and for the dinner invitation. It's really ok though. I'm glad you liked the painting, but I feel thanked enough. Dinner really isn't needed."

Janice smacked her. Charlotte silently yelled and rubbed her arm.

"So you don't want to go out to dinner with me?" Peter asked slowly.

"I do...I...I would love to," she stammered. "I just thought it was overkill for a painting and I didn't want to bother you or anything."

There was a pause and for a second, Charlotte thought she lost the call. She pulled the phone away from her ear for a second to double check that the call was still active then put the phone back to her ear.

"So, I'm going to cut to the chase here," Peter started slowly.

Did he really just say 'cut to the chase?' Do people really say that?

"I am really bad at asking women out. So bad it seems that when I am asking them out, they don't even realize I'm asking them out. So, I'm going to be really clear and put myself out on a limb...would you like to go out on a date with me?"

"Really?" Charlotte looked at Janice dumbfounded in the realization. Janice picked up on the look and smiled while doing a silent 'I told you so' dance.

"Um... yes...yes, I would like that a lot," Charlotte stammered.

Oh my God...yes I would like that a lot? What kind of moron are you?

"Alright. Great," Peter said. "I can be in town Friday night if that works for you. Say, 7pm?"

"Great. There's a nice Italian place on Fourth Avenue. Anthony's. Do you want to meet there?"

"It's a date."

The week flew by for Charlotte, assisted greatly by her new shoes, which she wore every day. She wanted to wear them in so she could wear them on Friday, but they really didn't need to be worn in they were so comfortable. Maybe she needed to start buying more expensive shoes. She always rolled her eyes a bit at Janice and her high end wardrobe, but maybe she had a point if expensive clothes were always so comfortable.

On Friday, she rushed out of work right at 5 rather than staying a little later and sorting one more pile or sending a few more emails as she normally did. She hopped in her car and was home in five minutes, having driven rather than riding today so she would have as much time as possible to figure out what to wear. Not that she needed to. She'd spent the entire week planning out her outfit.

By 6:40, she was in Anthony's parking lot. She'd gotten cleaned up and dressed in ten minutes and spent the next thirty pacing and trying to convince herself not to go, since it was only a five minute drive to the restaurant. Then she convinced herself there might be traffic, so she should be sure to arrive early. She sat in her car and started people watching. She thought about going in and grabbing a drink at the bar, but being twenty minutes early, she might get herself in some trouble having twenty minutes of nervous energy to calm with alcohol.

At 6:50, she started to worry. *What if he isn't coming? Was it 7pm? Oh my God...what if it was 6pm and he already left! I should go in and find out. How am I going to explain being almost an hour late? Anyone can make a mistake, right? Oh my God he's going to think I'm so stupid...can't even remember what time a date is!*

As she took off her seatbelt and grabbed her purse, ready to apologize for being so late *if he was still even there*, she heard the car next to her beep as the owner locked it. She hadn't even heard it park right next to her. Or had it already been there? She looked up and standing in front her was Peter, smiling with that same contemplative smile she remembered from the art show. He had his hands in his jeans pockets, with a similar polo and suit jacket to what she remembered him in before. *Signature look I guess.*

She smiled back and gave a little wave. He nodded back and stepped up to open her door.

"Charlotte Parker," he said as she stepped out of her car.

"Peter Li," she smiled back, glad she'd gone with the pants over the skirt. She somehow by some small miracle had managed to get out of the car with some amount of grace and she was fairly certain if she had worn the skirt she originally planned, there would have been a gust of wind, a puddle, and possibly a rabid dog attack just to complete her humiliation.

"I was finishing up a call when you parked and I was wondering how long you were going to sit in your car."

Humiliation achieved.

"Yeah, I have a bad habit of arriving early." Charlotte laughed at herself as they walked across the parking lot to the restaurant.

Might as well go all in.

"I was also really excited to see you, so, I'm surprised I was only twenty minutes early to be honest."

Peter paused at the restaurant door and shyly beamed. *Was he blushing? Did I just make someone blush?*

"Well I was excited to see you too."

They stood and smiled at each other for a minute before Peter reached toward her. For a split second, she thought he was leaning in for a kiss and she inhaled a little in anticipation before she realized he was just reaching over to open the door.

Damn.

The restaurant was more crowded than she thought and she was glad she'd made a reservation. Anthony's was a good place, but she'd never felt the need to make a reservation before. She'd just been so nervous something was going to go wrong she wanted to make sure they had a table. Apparently over thinking and over planning worked in her favor this time around.

"Must be a good place," Peter said as he took in the waiting diners.

"It is. I like it."

"I wonder if things are going to shut down here too."

"What do you mean?"

"You can't eat at a restaurant in New York right now. It's all takeout and delivery because of COVID."

Realization hit Charlotte. She'd been reading the news of course, but it was all happening so fast, she must have missed the restaurant shut down. But that was in New York. It probably wouldn't happen here.

She shook off the grim news and gave her name to the hostess who lead them right to a table in the corner. Charlotte couldn't remember the last time she had such a great date. Granted, she didn't have many others for comparison, but she defiantly couldn't remember one where all the nerves melted away in the first five minutes. Talking to Peter was so comfortable. The shoes made sense immediately...he did work for Thunderbolt in the city. Something in sales or dealing with international clients...Charlotte wasn't sure because she had found herself staring at him like a dreamy school girl at various points of the evening so she may have missed a detail or two. His mom and dad had owned a restaurant in Chinatown and after his dad died last summer, his mom had sold it and didn't want to live in the city anymore. He wished she still lived in the city so he could check in on her more often, but she was so happy where she was, so he had a hard time arguing with her. He had dated off and on, but admitted he spent his twenties working nonstop and before he realized it, he was 35 and still single, so he had made his first ever New Year's resolution (last year, he clarified, this was year two of said resolution which up to this point had been a colossal failure) and had purposely slowed down his pace at work to accommodate some kind of personal life.

They had finished their meal and second glasses of wine before Charlotte noticed the restaurant had filled up and there were people waiting.

"The restaurant is filling up," she said, slightly reluctantly. "We should probably free up the table."

Peter looked over his shoulder to the entrance.

"Oh wow, yeah. I was really enjoying our conversation so I didn't even notice."

Peter tossed his card in the sleeve of the little black booklet and the server grabbed it quickly. Apparently she was anxious to get rid of them and get a new table. Charlotte hoped she and Peter hadn't cost her too much in tips but couldn't help being a little annoyed they were being rushed out. Charlotte frantically tried to think of somewhere else to go so they could keep talking, but her mind was drawing a blank. There were coffee shops, but most of them were closed by this time. Any restaurant or bar would be loud and she really wanted to keep the conversation going.

The server was back at the table faster than Charlotte thought was possible and Peter signed the slip and returned his card to his wallet while Charlotte's mind raced, trying to figure out where they could go.

"Do you want to come back to my house for some coffee or something?"

Oh my God.

Had she just done that? Seriously, it had been a nice evening, but this guy could still be a serial killer. Ted Bundy was super charming and good looking, right? She started planning escape routes out of her own house...

She really needed to stop watching real crime shows.

Peter smiled.

"I would love that."

She flashed a smile bigger than she intended but he flashed one to match, so embarrassment was quickly replaced with sheer joy.

God he is good looking.

The server started clearing the table as soon as they stood up and they walked to the door, Peter lightly placing his hand on the small of Charlotte's back just long enough for her to melt slightly. When they got through the small crowd of waiting diners and he took his hand back, Charlotte fought the urge to turn around so he could guide her through the crowd again and get his hand back. They got in their cars and Peter followed her home. Charlotte started panicking. Had she just invited a guy home on the first date? Was he expecting sex now? Not that that would be the worst thing...Steve was the last one and that was, what, a year ago already? Still, first date? But there was no guarantee, right? He did have garlic pesto, which is a pretty bold first date choice, so maybe that was a signal that he wasn't expecting anything.

Stop it. He hasn't been playing games with you all night. Why would he start now? Or was he playing games? Ugh...adulting sucks.

Charlotte pulled into her garage and Peter pulled in the driveway. She got out and stood by the garage door while Peter got out and walked up to her. He ran his hand through his hair as he approached and a few strands fell right back into place over his right eye. *God he's good looking.*

Charlotte gestured for him to follow her in through the garage, but as she turned to go, he lightly grabbed her elbow and turned her back.

"So under the heading of being really bad at this and wanting to cut to the chase, "

Cut to the chase...yes he really does like that phrase.

"I'm not expecting anything, and I don't know if you're expecting anything. Like I told you earlier, I don't date much, I don't want to play games, I don't want misunderstandings. I like you. I don't think I've ever been more comfortable with anyone so quickly. I just want openness and honesty, and I think I've gotten that from you so far, so I'd like that to continue."

Charlotte looked at him in near shock. She hadn't expected so much to suddenly come pouring out of him, and it was shockingly refreshing. The thing she hated the most about dating was the unknown. Trying to decide what someone meant by what they said rather than just listening to what they said. Why couldn't all relationships be like this?

The shock melted into a smile.

"That's exactly how I feel."

His slightly concerned expression morphed into a genuine smile and Charlotte melted.

God he's good looking.

She tried to pull herself away to head inside, but she was suddenly very aware of how close they were in that moment. She took a slight step back, repositioning herself against her car door as they looked at each other in silence. Charlotte took notice of every inch of his face, now only a few inches away from hers, watching the smile turn into something more serious. She felt herself start breathing more deliberately, matching the slow mood shift from a break in tension to a new, exciting anticipation.

It all seemed to happen in slow motion, Charlotte's breathing getting heavier and Peter moved in closer to her, stepping toward her until his body gently pushed hers against the car door. She instinctively lifted her chin and met his lips as Peter made the final move in to her. She let herself enjoy the release of joy in that moment, refusing to let it end by lightly running her hands around him and pulling him even closer. She felt his hands come to rest on her waist, and her heart raced as the slow motion fell away. Neither one of their hands stayed in place as they started exploring each other, and Charlotte took her first deep inhale as Peter's lips found their way to her neck. Her hand shot up his back and neck, meeting his hairline and encouraging him to continue his exploration as she felt his hand wrap around her waist, pulling her away from her car just enough to clear a path for his hand's journey south. The shyness that had encircled them a few minutes earlier was replaced with ever increasing forcefulness as Charlotte let her free hand skate the length of Peters arm, feeling his bicep flex as he pulled her closer and cupped her backside, squeezing hard enough that she audibly gasped.

Peter pulled away, still holding her tightly but searching her face for a sign…permission to continue or an immediate halt.

Charlotte caught her breath and looked at Peter. She felt him loosen his grasp on her slightly and she gently lowered her hands. Peter's face fell slightly as he lightly cleared his throat, and Charlotte could tell he was worried he had overstepped his bounds, as she gently guided the two of them apart. He stepped back, gathering himself and looking ready to say good night, but Charlotte let her hands rest in his, and took a few steps backwards towards her door, pulling him gently along, and enjoying watching his handsome face change expressions.

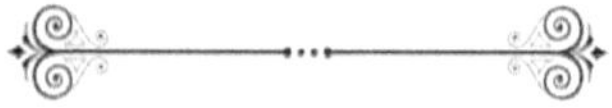

The next morning, Charlotte woke up and rolled over, expecting to cuddle up but finding nothing but a pillow that smelled like Peter's aftershave. For a horrible moment, she thought everything they had talked about last night had been a lie and he really had just wanted a one night stand. The fears were quickly put down as Peter entered the room with two cups of coffee.

"Nice robe," Charlotte commented as Peter laughed at himself, having borrowed her purple flowery bathrobe that she very rarely used herself.

"I thought it was a winning look," he said as he sat on the bed and handed her a cup of coffee.

"I saw creamer in the fridge so I assumed. How'd I do on your coffee order?"

"Perfect," she half lied. She usually dropped an ice cube in so she didn't burn her taste buds every morning, but this was pretty close and she didn't work today, so she could let it cool off.

"So it looks like I am going to be in town for a while. Governor Cuomo closed the schools and we aren't supposed to have people in the office unless it's absolutely necessary, so we're all working from home."

Charlotte inhaled slightly. Obviously everyone had been following news of the pandemic, and she'd been reading and watching the news like everyone else. Her boss had put out the order a few days ago for the entire district to start working on remote plans, so she'd been working on plans for the library in case they had to shut down, but it was all theoretical. Knowing that New York just shut down made things in Vermont seem much more likely. No wonder Anthony's was so busy last night. The entire town may have been trying to get in one last night out.

"Are you still going to work?" Charlotte asked with concern. She didn't worry too much about herself. Because of her father's buyout from Parker Marketing and the fact that she owned her home outright, even if she was suddenly out of work she'd be fine for months, but she didn't really know much about Peter's job and she was worried he'd suddenly be out of a job, which was a growing concern the news pundits were talking about.

"No, I'm fine. Most of what I do can be done remotely. I'm definitely worried about some of the lower level employees, but hopefully this doesn't last too long."

"Do you need to go home and get things?"

"No actually. We've been working on the remote plan for the last month so I basically have everything I need at my mom's. I've actually been working out of her house off and on so I guess that's my permanent office for the duration."

Charlotte smiled and sipped her coffee. *Still too hot!* While a pandemic was certainly not anything to be glad about, she found herself extremely relieved to know Peter would be safe and in town. She was really looking forward to seeing more of him.

Not that there's much more of him to see she thought as he readjusted how he was sitting on the bed and the purple floral robe opened a bit.

2004

Charlotte watched the trees go by. It was amazing how trees all looked the same, but she could still tell that these trees were the ones exactly 5 minutes away from the cabin. She took the bookmark out from the last few pages of the book she was reading and marked her page before putting the book back in her backpack and reaching for her shoes.

"How many books did you bring for the weekend?" her dad asked while taking a sip of coffee from his travel mug.

"Like, seven. I'm almost done with one so, six and a half I guess."

"Are you going to finish them all this weekend?" he asked as he turned the wheel and they turned onto the long, winding road that lead to the cabin.

"Probably," she answered as she finished tying her shoes.

"Maybe try spending a little more time with your cousins this year."

Charlotte shot her father a confused look. He took a breath and gathered his thoughts.

"I know the past few years have been hard since mom died. I know it's been an adjustment and we've both been dealing with it in our own ways. You've just been very quiet since then...lost in books."

"I like reading."

"And that's great Charlie. I love how much you read and how smart you are. I just want you to understand how important your family is. Especially since we moved out of the city, we don't see everyone as often as we used to, so you can really use this time to get to know your cousins better."

Charlotte sat back and thought about what her father was saying. She hadn't enjoyed the last several reunions aside from laying in the hammock on the second story balcony and reading. Most of the family stayed in the main part of the house, or went out boating or swimming in the lake, so she felt like she had her own little hiding place in a house full of people. George was 22 now, and Elizabeth 21. They'd always stayed mostly with the adults anyway. From as far back as she could remember, George and Elizabeth had always been 'adults', even when they were kids. Charles and William were both at Yale, and it seemed all they did last year was talk to her dad about all things Yale related which Charlotte quickly tired of. Travis and Trevor had both left high school a few years ago and finished GEDs with a tutor while they started modeling at the same agency Aunt Ana modeled for. At 19, Travis had taken the previous year off and had spent a lot of time at some clinic in Arizona, where Aunt Ana said he was doing very well. Charlotte didn't really know what that meant. Maybe there was some medical school in Arizona he was going to. Trevor had started getting small acting jobs. She and her father had watched him on some cop show where he was playing an informant or a drug dealer or something. Charlotte hadn't really paid attention to the show, although she had thought it was funny to see 'Trev Parker' in the opening credits. Apparently he had shortened his name for his upcoming movie career. She had heard her father on the phone talking to Uncle Luke about it but he had never sounded really happy about it.

Maybe this was the teenage angst she'd heard so many adults talking about. She wasn't there yet (she turned 13 in November) so she was close. Adults were always talking about how teenagers were difficult and sullen and impossible. Maybe she was just ahead of the rest of the kids in her class and she was already all those things. Maybe it was her fault she hadn't enjoyed anything aside from reading.

"I will dad."

That answer seemed to please him well enough as he turned onto the familiar winding road to the cottage. Charlotte zipped up her backpack and finished tying her shoes as her dad parked and the staff came down the steps to grab the bags.

Grandma Evelyn came out to greet them as she always did with her outstretched arms and a hug. Charlotte pulled he in close and swore she was smaller than she was last year. Of course she'd grown three inches over the past year, so maybe it was her imagination.

"Charlotte dear, " Grandma started. "All the little ones went in for a swim. Why don't you change into your bathing suit and go join them. They just replaced the floating diving platform and there's a new ladder that is easier to get up on."

Charlotte didn't want to go swimming. She was at a good part of her book and really just wanted to finish it before dinner. However, she'd promised her dad she'd try to spend more time with her cousins, and, she did have a new bathing suit she really liked, so there really wasn't an excuse. She smiled and nodded before heading up to the loft.

On her way down the stairs after a quick change into the new green and black striped swimsuit, she heard someone talking in angry tones. She slowed down and quietly looked over the railing to see what was happening. Uncle Luke and Aunt Ana were there with her father, Aunt Ana's arms folded in front of her and Uncle Luke pointing an accusing finger at him.

"You said you were taking care of it!"

"And I am Luke, but there's only so much I can do," her father said in a calm, measured tone.

"Trevor needs this shit off his record. If the studio finds out they might drop him"

"And I'm working on it," Charlotte's father said calmly. "The arrest is buried and I think I can argue it down out of court, but if I can't he's going to have to make a court appearance and it's going to be public."

"We can't do that," said Aunt Ana. "He might be able to weather something like this later in his career but it'll end him now."

Charlotte watched her father bury his frustration.

"He can always just go back to school."

Both Luke and Ana shook their heads.

"No that's not happing," said Luke.

"He should have a degree," reasoned her father, his frustration boiling over for a brief moment. "Most people need proper job training and modeling and acting aren't exactly the most stable career paths."

"Yeah and most people don't have the Parker name behind them," hissed Luke.

The three of them stood in silence for a minute, before Luke took out a cigarette and headed for the back deck.

"Fix it John!"

Charlotte sat back on the step as her father exhaled loudly and headed to the kitchen with Aunt Ana. Charlotte stepped down the rest of the stairs quickly, holding her beach towel tightly and making her way down to the lake.

At the edge of the water, her cousin Elizabeth sat in a deck chair, sunning herself and listening to her iPod. She had a navy blue bikini that matched the navy and white stripped towel she had dropped over the chair, with her blonde hair pulled up into a perfect bun on top of our head. She was stunningly beautiful, looking like she was ready for a magazine cover shoot in that very moment. Charlotte looked down at her own suit, a green and black striped one piece she just got for the start of swim season. The high neck and racer back was great for competitive swimming, but maybe she should have rethought it for fun swimming in the lake.

She draped her towel over the fence near the water line and took off her sandals. Elizabeth hadn't noticed her arrival and Charlotte didn't want to bother her. She looked out across the lake and saw William and Charles race each other off the diving platform and jump into the water. Beyond that, George was treading water and saying something to them she couldn't quite make out. Travis was laying on his back on the diving platform smoking a cigarette. She looked around for Trevor but couldn't see him. She took a few steps towards the water before she was suddenly swept off her feet and flying towards the lake. She managed a small yelp before looking back at who she had flung her arms around. Trevor laughed as the water started splashing up around them, before slowing down as the lake deepened to his thighs. He stopped and started swinging Charlotte back and forth.

"One...Two...God how much do you weigh Charlotte?... THREE!!!!"

With a mighty heave, Trevor launched his cousin into the water where she ungracefully cannonballed. The force of hitting thigh deep water drove her straight to the bottom, where an unusually large and unfortunately sharp rock greeted her. She screamed in pain, getting a mouthful of lake water in the process. She tried to readjust herself and push up but ended up hitting the same rock in the exact some spot on her butt. She desperately kicked herself to the side, her bruised backside sending a shot of pain all the way down her leg, before she managed to sit herself up, coughing and gasping for air.

In between her gasps of oxygen, she heard the clapping and cheering of her cousins. She wiped water off her face and looked up. Trevor was taking a bow.

"Ready for the Olympic diving team Charlotte!" William called out.

"Perfect ten!" George echoed.

Charlotte sat and sputtered for another few seconds as Trevor waded further out into the lake, joining the rest of the Parker crew. She leaned heavily on her right side while her left throbbed and she let her leg float. She watched her cousins swim and talk, pull themselves up on the diving platform and then jump off, laugh and enjoy each other's company. She spent so much time alone with her dad, watching people loudly roughhouse and laugh was almost like watching a nature show. She studied them, not understanding how they related to each other. How was she supposed to join in with them? She was a strong swimmer, (although not overly fast, as her swim coach lamented) but as she watched her cousins swim, dive, and dunk each other, she wasn't sure she wanted to join in.

But she'd promised her dad.

She started to readjusted herself so she could stand up and immediately regretted it. She sat back down in the water and thought about swimming out to them so she didn't have to walk, but as she flipped over and started swimming in the shallow water, she quickly realized she would have to swim with one leg, which was not something she was willing to do to get out to the roughhousing young men in the middle of the lake. She looked back towards the shore where Elizabeth was still laying on the beach chair. It wasn't that far. She could make it. She didn't really have a choice, did she? She had to get out of the lake at some point.

One painful step after the next, she hobbled out of the lake, wincing with every step of her left leg and watching her towel hanging on the fence getting closer, although it wasn't getting closer very quickly. After what seemed like a ten mile hike up the lake shore, she got to her towel and wrapped herself up.

Then she glanced up at the house.

It might as well have been a thousand miles away.

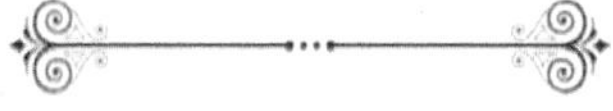

Charlotte had stayed in her room until dinner. By the time she made it up to the loft room her and her father shared, she couldn't hold the tears back and her cheeks were soaked. She showered and checked her reflection in the full length mirror on the door of the bathroom. Her entire backside was turning a fascinating shade of purple. She had tried to put on her nice jeans to go down for dinner, but she couldn't pull them up over the bruise, so she put her sweatpants on instead. Grandma wouldn't appreciate sweatpants at the dinner table, but Charlotte decided sweatpants were better than no pants.

At 6:30, she started hobbling down the stairs for dinner. Her family was sitting in the living room, drinking wine and scotch while Lindsey set the table and ran back and forth between the dining table and the kitchen. She limped down the last step and started across the living room trying to walk as evenly as possible. She went over to the sofa and sat carefully on the soft cushion.

"Look who finally decided to join us!" exclaimed William

Charlotte smiled shyly and everyone went back to their conversations and drinks. Her father sat down next to Charlotte and spoke quietly to her.

"What's with the sweats Charlotte?"

"I just couldn't get my jeans on," she said embarrassed.

He exhaled audibly.

"You really should have put something nicer on for dinner."

"I know dad. I'm sorry."

He took a sip of his wine and looked at her for a second before a small smile crossed his face.

"Its ok Charlie. But I want you out and about tomorrow. No hiding in our room. And nice clothes for dinner and for church on Sunday."

Charlotte nodded. That seemed to satisfy him and he smiled, tapped her knee and got up. Charlotte screamed inwardly at the shot of pain the gentle tap sent streaming through her leg but managed to keep in all to herself. She didn't have long to scream however, as Lindsey called everyone over for dinner.

At the dinner table, Charlotte sat as straight as she could, but still ended up looking like the leaning tower of Pisa. The one thing she was grateful for in the moment was Lindsey's cooking. She hadn't had lunch earlier because the idea of coming back down the stairs had been too much at the time, so she was ready to chew her own arm off. She stared at her plate while Grandpa said grace, willing the food into her stomach and wishing her grandfather had a little less to say to the Lord at the moment. When the long awaited 'Amen' finally came she immediately dug into her potatoes, taking two quick forkfuls and wishing it would get to her stomach faster.

"Having a little to eat there, Charlotte?" her Uncle Mark asked loud enough for the whole table to hear. She froze her chewing, suddenly very aware that her cheeks were currently potato puffs. Uncle Mark puffed his cheeks out and made a few chewing motions to the delight of those around the table. A general guffaw rang out as he pushed his belly out and rubbed it. Charlotte looked down at her plate, desperate to eat in peace, but everyone's attention had been directed towards her now. She had to get the attention off her. As carefully as she could, she sent small bits of potato to her waiting stomach, trying to pinch her cheeks in as she did. As soon as the attention had been turned on her, it was off again, and she spent the rest of the meal quietly taking small bites of a green bean. Just enough to keep her stomach from growling. By the time Lindsey was clearing the table, Charlotte had only made it through a small fraction of her plate. She watched Lindsey take the plate back in the kitchen and winced inwardly as the remaining food was dumped in the trash.

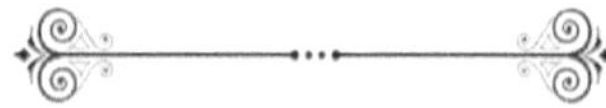

By Saturday morning, the bruise covered most of her backside. She found a comfortable position on the hammock on the back porch and spent most of the morning there reading, politely declining invitations from her family to put her swimsuit on and join them on the big boat. Having everyone out gave her a chance to eat breakfast in peace, which turned into a mistake. Having not really eaten a full meal in 24 hours, she ate a lot of food really fast and ended up laying in the hammock in pain as her stomach struggled to digest.

Around 1:30, the doorbell rang. It took Charlotte totally by surprise and she almost fell out of the hammock. Who would be ringing the doorbell? The only people who came up to the cottage were the family. It's not as if this was a place someone 'happened' upon. She waited and strained to hear Lindsey open the door before she remembered Lindsey had joined the family on the boat so they could have lunch on the water. The doorbell rang a second time. Right...she was the only one in the house. Charlotte poured herself out of the hammock and limped towards the door. When she finished her endless trek to the other side of the cottage, having sped up as much as she could when the doorbell rang a third time, she finally arrived at the front door.

On the other side of the front door, Charlotte was greeted by a lone woman. Wrapped in a fur, she stood perfectly posed and flashed a million dollar smile. She had a perfect collection of blonde hair wrapped on top of her head, and the most stunning magazine quality make up Charlotte had ever seen.

"Is this the Parker residence?" She asked, snapping Charlotte out of her trance.

"Um, yes," she stuttered.

"Oh thank goodness!" the woman said, unwrapping her fur and gliding into the house past Charlotte.

"I thought it would be nice to drive myself up and I got completely lost," she giggled slightly at herself and dropped the fur towards Charlotte, who somehow magically managed to catch it. "I should have known better than to drive up alone but what's life without a little adventure now and then?"

Charlotte stood by the open door, holding the coat which had landed in her arms in such a way that the animal's head stared at her judgmentally, wondering what had just happened. Not really knowing what else to do, Charlotte closed the front door and slowly followed the mystery woman into the living room.

"Oh this is charming, isn't it? Margaret and Julia told me it was a charming little place. I see why they like it so. Would you mind getting me a glass of wine dear? I am so frazzled after that drive I just need to relax a minute!"

Charlotte stood still, holding the coat and cocking her head to the side slightly, not sure how to respond. She glanced towards the kitchen. She knew where the wine was, and she could get it for her, but should she? Sometimes she grabbed drinks for her Uncles when they were playing cards. They used to pay her a dime for running glasses back to the kitchen when she was little. She looked back at the mystery woman and realized the woman was looking at her for the first time since Charlotte had opened the door.

"My goodness you look young. How long have you been with the Parkers?"

Charlotte's brow furrowed. What was she talking about? She'd been with the Parkers her whole life. Assuming honesty was the best policy, she answered truthfully.

"Twelve years."

"Twelve years? How in the world..." mystery woman trailed off, a wave a realization coming over her.

"Are you Charlotte?"

Charlotte nodded.

Mystery woman laughed at herself, her hands covering her cheeks gracefully before clasping each other in front of her small waist.

"My dear, I am so sorry. I am so frazzled after my drive I didn't put two and two together. Let me take that back," she said as she stepped forward and took her coat back, gracefully draping it over her arm.

"I'm a friend of your Aunt Margaret and Aunt Julia. They invited me up for the weekend. I'm Jennifer Ferguson."

Charlotte quietly said hello and looked her up and down as she started talking and crossed the room to the sofa, draping her coat over the back of it. She was rambling on about traffic or something Charlotte didn't really care to listen to. She was wearing a form fitting skirt, high heels, and a well-tailored cream sweater. Her blonde hair was up in a flawless bun, and her makeup was just enough to show she was wearing it, but not so much that she looked overly made up.

Charlotte was suddenly very aware of her ratty ponytail, sweatpants, and swollen backside.

"...don't you think dear?" Jennifer asked. Charlotte hadn't been listening and stared blankly at her, desperately trying to think of something to say. Just as the silence was getting awkward, the back door opened and her family trooped in from their morning on the lake. Aunt Margaret and Aunt Julia opened their arms as wide as their smiles and greeted their friend before ushering her to the sofa as Lindsey went to the kitchen to grab drinks for everyone. Charles and William buzzed past her, probably to change clothes upstairs. Elizabeth joined her mother greeting the guest, while Travis and Trevor flopped down on the sofa and pulled out their cell phones. (There was barely any service in the cottage but there was less on the lake)

"You missed a nice morning on the boat Charlotte," her cousin George said as he walked past her to head upstairs. Uncle Matthew and her father were helping Grandpa George into the big chair in the corner. He let out a big sigh as he landed, looking obviously worn out from the morning. Charlotte had noticed her grandfather looking old this year, although at 84, he was hardly young. Grandma Evelyn fussed over him a little more than she used to, and he didn't join in the conversations like he used to. It was a strange thing for her to watch.

"John," Julia called from across the room, gracefully ushering Jennifer toward Charlotte's father. "You remember Jennifer Howard."

"No no." she interrupted with a smile. "All the paperwork is in, I'm back to Jenifer Ferguson now."

"Of course," John smiled and shook her hand.

"I met up with her for lunch last week and the poor thing was saying her trip to Prague got postponed at the last minute, so the deary didn't have anywhere to go for Labor Day weekend. I thought we'd be able to show her a bit of fun," Julia said as she nudged Jennifer a little closer.

John took a half step back and opened his arms a bit.

"Well, we aren't Prague, but as you can see, there's nowhere better to be for Labor Day."

Lindsey arrived and started handing around wine glasses while everyone talked about who was doing what in the city and other things that seemed to require endless amounts of discussion. Eventually, card games accompanied the conversations, dinner was served over more conversations, and Charlotte managed to finish her book while what she swore was the same conversation was still happening.

Charlotte didn't get a break from the conversation the next morning as the family piled into cars to go to church. Aunt Julia and Aunt Margaret seemed to have an endless amount of things to say to Jennifer, but they kept insisting on placing Charlotte's dad in between them and talking over him rather than sitting together. The conversation finally had to take a break during the service but was replaced by the droning on of the preacher while Charlotte tried to sit straight on her bruised backside. She did her best not to squirm, knowing how important church was to her grandparents and wanting to please them, but she could feel every beat of her heart course through her bruise and all she wanted to do was cry. She distracted herself by looking around at the congregation. It was a strange thing to look at a group of people that she didn't know but still knew really well. She knew the 'lake people' because they all owned the properties around the lake and lived in buildings near each other in the city. Charlotte saw them periodically at restaurants when she and her father were in the city because they would come up to speak to her father, grandparents, or Aunts and Uncles. They all had their assigned seats here in the church. There were some kids her age that she recognized from jumping off the decks of their family boats out in the middle of the lake. All the adults seemed to know everything about each other, and Charlotte had little nicknames for them she kept to herself since it was easier than actually remembering all their names.

She glanced around and let her eyes rest on The Ancient Ones, the older couple who seemed to have been born as an elderly couple, Lord and Lady Hamptons, who always talked about their other home in the Hamptons, and finally The Pointer Sisters, the two ladies with the sharp features that made them look like animated villains. Normally, everyone's attention was on the preacher, but she noticed as she looked around the congregation, she noticed glances toward her. She was suddenly very self conscience, until she realized the glances weren't really at her, but just past her. She followed some of the glances back to her father sitting next to her. Having been raised in a very religious household, he was focused on the sermon, something Charlotte found strange every time they went to church, since they only went when they were with Charlotte's grandparents. Still, he always paid close attention to the sermons, and today was no different. What was different was the woman sitting next to him. Jennifer sat next to him, her legs crossed in the pew in just such a way that she leaned slightly toward him. She had a slight smile on her face as she watched the sermon, but Charlotte noticed her eyes drifting ever so slightly around the sanctuary, taking in the glances of the other members of the congregation.

Charlotte had never really seen her dad as anything other than her dad, but suddenly, he was just a good looking forty two year old single man, sitting next to a woman who looked like she just walked right off the runway and took a seat. She supposed this was bound to happen, but she wasn't sure how she felt about it. She looked at the two of them, her father in a well-tailored suit, Jennifer in a perfectly fitted dress, and then looked down at her own, lumpy sweater and oversized skirt.

Something here didn't belong, and Charlotte felt like she knew what it was.

Chapter 6

It had been the weirdest month of Charlotte's life.

A week after Peter moved into his 'northern extension office' as he called it, Vermont had basically shut down and suddenly Charlotte was working from home too. It wasn't as drastic as New York, but they didn't have anywhere near as many COVID cases. Still, most of the town was shut down and Charlotte and the rest of the library staff started working from home, going into work one at a time to collect online book orders, record fun videos for the community and restock returned material in silence that was weird, even in a library. Anytime Charlotte was in, she actually blasted music over the intercom just for some company.

Peter stayed at his mom's, locked up in his makeshift office, but always came over to Charlotte's for dinner, usually proclaiming 'Honey, I'm home!' in his best 1950's tv voice. He usually had to go back to his mom's for additional meetings or phone calls, but after a few days, he started bringing things over so he could finish his work at Charlotte's and stay the night. It only took ten days before the northern extension office had fully relocated to Charlotte's guest room.

By the third week of April, they had a regular routine going...Sunday, morning sex followed by breakfast made by Charlotte and then a movie or

Netflix binge. Monday, Tuesday, and Wednesday, office hours and evening sex like sensible people. Thursday, dinner with Peter's mom followed by delayed evening sex so they had time to digest. Friday, Peter worked at home while Charlotte had her shift at the library. Then date night, which consisted of wine and whatever food Peter found in the kitchen served on the kitchen table with the fancy tablecloth Charlotte wasn't too sure why she owned. Then sex. Saturday, lunch at Charlotte's dad's, followed by a movie or card game they usually didn't finish.

The early stages of a relationship are really quite a marathon.

One Friday near the end of April, Charlotte was working her shift putting books away and dancing to Britney Spears (since no one was there to judge her) when she heard a banging at the front door. She walked toward the circulation desk and saw Peter standing outside. They waved at each other and she ducked behind the counter to stop her phone and click off the intercom. She went over and unlocked the door, greeting Peter with a big smile and a kiss.

"What are you doing here?" she said as she relocked the door behind him.

"I just needed to check on what you oops, did again," he said teasingly.

"Shut up."

"No no," he said in a mock serious tone. "I know you, and you're not that innocent," he said, singing the last three words in his best Britney Spears impersonation.

Charlotte rolled her eyes and lead him into her office where they plopped down on the couch.

Charlotte propped herself up on the arm of the couch with a pillow and swung her legs onto Peter's lap, her favorite Netflix watching position.

"So you don't get enough of me at home? You're bothering me at work too?"

"Yeah I just had kind of a rough couple of meetings this morning and I wanted to come see you."

"I'm sorry. Do you want to talk about it?"

"Not really. I spent the morning talking about it."

"Ok. Name a different topic. We'll talk about that." She said, taking up a more optimistic tone.

"Let's talk about us," he said, settling himself into the couch.

"I hope that's a pleasant topic."

"I think it is," Peter said, putting his hand on her leg which Charlotte had flung over his lap.

"I do too."

The two of them sat quietly for a minute, Peter gently rubbing her leg and keeping his gaze down, almost like he was watching his hand move. She hated seeing him like this. She gave him a few minutes to collect himself, knowing he'd start when he was ready and had fully formed what he wanted to say.

"Is it just me," he started "or does all of this seem too easy?"

Charlotte took a breath in and cocked her head. "It does seem to be a little easy, doesn't it. Are you suggesting we have a fight?"

"I guess we could try it, but it doesn't sound like a lot of fun."

"Nah, I'm not a fan."

"Alright we won't do that," Peter said as he stroked her thigh.

Charlotte hadn't seen him this contemplative for a while. Occasionally, she could tell he'd had a rough day at work and he would get quiet and especially cuddly with her. She really didn't understand the business world. Even though her extended family were all into big business in the city, always talking about it, Charlotte had never really picked up on any of it. Maybe she should have listened more. Maybe it would help her help Peter deal with whatever he was dealing with.

Or, maybe her lack of business knowledge was a good thing right now. Maybe a distraction from his day to day life was exactly what he needed. Maybe he needed the topic change.

"Well what do you suggest instead?" she said lightheartedly, ready to discuss plot points on The Office or whether or not Bigfoot really was just the best at playing hide and seek, a debate they had had many times.

"What's your opinion on marriage?"

Charlotte froze. She had been so relaxed a second ago. She was just sitting on the couch with her boyfriend. Actually, they had never really called each other 'boyfriend' and 'girlfriend'. They hadn't even discussed it. Now, they are casually sitting on the couch and he just throws the word 'marriage' out there like he's asking what she wants for dinner? What the hell just happened?

She inhaled slowly, choosing her next words carefully.

"Generally speaking," she started slowly, "I'm in favor of the institution."

After a pause that seemed to stretch into eternity, she decided to go for the big question.

"Why?"

"Just wondering," he said calmly. "Why?" he added slowly with a sideways glance in her direction.

Oh my God...why? Why did I ask that?!?!?!

Charlotte's mind and heart raced. Was this really a conversation she was having? Was he proposing right now? Was that actually what was happening right now? Was that what she wanted right now? She was prepared to talk about Bigfoot or TV shows. She was not prepared to have a major life conversation sitting in her office on a Friday afternoon.

"It just seemed like a big question," she said slowly.

"But it wasn't a big question," he said calmly turning his gaze back towards the office door. They sat in silence for a few beats, Peter slowly running his hand over her thigh, Charlotte trying to slow her well above average heart rate.

Peter inhaled deeply and sat up a little straighter on the couch. Charlotte's entire being stood still. He turned towards her more fully.

"Were you hoping it was a big question?"

Her gut reaction was a resounding 'YES!!!' but that was quickly thwarted by the more mature voice of reason. Still, she took a few breaths and chose her words.

"It's only been a month, so the most reasonable thing is to keep things as they are and see what happens."

Peter nodded and looked back towards the office door. Charlotte felt her heart pounding in every part of her body. They sat together in silence for what felt like an hour but in reality was probably no more than a minute. Charlotte's mouth gaped slightly as she tried to get enough oxygen into her system to calm herself down. Finally, quietly, Peter brought his eyes toward her without actually looking at her.

"And if I was asking?"

YES!!!!! YES!!!!!! OH MY GOD YES!!!!!! Charlotte screamed as she flung her arms around him, kissed him deeply, and then danced around her office as she named their children...

In her mind.

Once again, sensible, reasoned Charlotte beat impulsive Charlotte down within seconds, bringing her back to the reality of what was happening. She took a deep breath, steadied herself, and spoke as calmly as she could muster.

"I want nothing more than for you to ask me, but it's only been a month. It's more sensible to keep things as they are and see what happens."

Peter smiled, with a strange mix of sadness, pride in Charlotte, and something she couldn't quite put her finger on. He leaned forward, and Charlotte took her legs down off his lap. He reached for her, cupping her head gently and drawing her in for a deep kiss. When it ended, they pulled back and looked at each other for a long moment, before cuddling up with Charlotte's head on his shoulder and Peter wrapping his arm around her. They sat like that for a long time, just sitting in the moment and both digesting what had just been discussed. After a few minutes,

Charlotte picked her head up off Peter's shoulder and they looked at each other.

"What would you have done if I had said yes?"

Peter gave that smirky smile Charlotte had come to know and love over the last month when he teased her.

"I guess I would have married you."

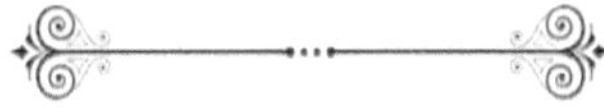

In the first week of May, Janice had texted Charlotte that she was officially fed up and needed to see people. Frankly, Charlotte was surprised it had taken this long. Everyone was suffering a little from 'quarantine fatigue' and for a social butterfly like Janice, it had to be extra excruciating. Charlotte thought texting and phone calls were enough, but Janice insisted on some face time, so she decided to set up a weekly virtual chat with her, Hannah, and Katie so they could all see each other drink wine and talk about how nothing new was going on. At first, Charlotte thought it was kind of ridiculous, but she sat herself down at her desk with a glass of wine, and after a few minutes of talking to her friends and actually seeing their faces, she understood why Janice wanted to do this. Janice would run games, they would leave bottles of wine on each other's porches to try on the chat, and generally be goofy. Charlotte actually started looking forward to each meeting. Through May and June, they started moving the meetings to a socially distanced backyard gathering, usually at Katie or Hannah's house so they didn't have to leave the kids if their husbands were out.

After a few minutes of giggles and day drinking stories at the last meeting in July, which had to move back online due to rain, Hannah got down to business.

"Ok, so Charlotte, did Janice get it wrong, or are you actually living with a man none of us has actually met?"

Charlotte felt her cheeks burn and she tried to hide it by taking another drink.

"Oh yes," started Janice, "she moved in with the man. But if someone asked me out with Thunderbolt shoes I would probably move in with him too."

"Come on Char, spill it. I want all the details," said Katie.

Charlotte relented. It had been nice having the relationship all to herself, but she supposed it was inevitable it was going to come out eventually. She was actually surprised she'd been able to hide it four whole months without having to spill too much, but it had been an odd four months so it hadn't been difficult for other topics of conversation to take priority over her love life.

"Ok, ok...his name is Peter, he works at Thuderbolt in New York, but his mom lives here in town. We met at the library art show back in March when he stopped in while he was visiting his mom. We started seeing each other and when things started shutting down, he was here and he set up his remote office at his mom's. He started spending so much time at my house he just kinda...moved in."

Hannah looked at her in shock.

"Who are you?" she laughed

Charlotte laughed back.

"I admit, its very out of character, but honestly, everything has just felt right."

"That's how you know. I was so comfy with Matt when we first got together. He was the first guy I could just be myself with," Janice said

"C'mon...is he home? I wanna meet him!" begged Hannah.

"Yes yes yes!!" said Janice and Katie in unison.

Charlotte sighed and looked back toward the kitchen. Peter had been in a meeting earlier, but he was in the kitchen now putting dishes away from the dishwasher. She supposed there was no putting this off any longer. She called back to him.

"Hey. Do you have a second to meet my friends?"

Peter looked up and smiled. He put the plate in his hand away and came over to Charlotte's desk, crouching down next to her to get his face in frame.

"Hey ladies. I'm Peter. Nice to meet you."

Katie and Hannah introduced themselves and started peppering him with questions. Peter smiled through the inquisition and was exceedingly charming. Charlotte couldn't figure out why she had wanted to hide him. He obviously liked being shown off to her circle of friends and she loved showing him off.

Peter allowed himself to be grilled for the next few minutes and then cleverly used a lull to excuse himself so they could 'let Charlotte know what they really thought.' He stood and gave her a quick peck on the forehead before heading off to the spare bedroom to give Charlotte some privacy.

"Ok, " Charlotte started. "what do you think?"

"Oh my God, Char...LOVE HIM!!" said Hannah.

"So cute," Katie followed up. "And funny!"

"I'm so jealous," said Hannah. "I mean, don't get me wrong, I love my husband, Jeff is an amazing man and an awesome dad, but holy moly Charlotte. Damn!"

Charlotte felt her face flush again and this time, didn't try to hide it. Hannah, Katie, and Janice were all married and Charlotte had basically been single through all their love stories, so it felt good to be the one in focus for once. She looked back and forth at Katie and Hannah as they continued to compliment Peter, but when she focused on Janice, she noticed her looking down at a stack of magazines, quickly glancing at one before moving on to the next. Suddenly, she seemed to find what she was looking for and quickly turned pages in the magazine she had selected.

"Janice?" Charlotte started. "Everything ok?"

"What's Peter's middle name?' Janice asked, without looking up, and still flipping pages.

"James," Charlotte answered, confused as to why Janice was suddenly being so uncharacteristically serious. Janice stopped short in the magazine and gasped. In unison, Katie, Hannah, and Charlotte asked what she was looking at.

"I thought I recognized him," Janice looked up at her screen. "Charlotte, why didn't you tell me you were dating P.J. Li?"

"P.J.?" Charlotte laughed at the idea of calling Peter 'P.J.' "I did tell you we were dating. You were there when I called him."

"No," Janice corrected. "You told me you were dating Peter who works at Thunderbolt. You never said you were dating P.J. Freaking Li, the CEO of Thunderbolt."

With that, she held the magazine up to the screen, and there was Peter, with a giant headline, '40 under 40 to watch...P.J. Li, number 14'. Hannah and Katie both gasped and started talking at once. Charlotte tried to process what she was seeing. She read quite a bit obviously but tended not to read magazines. Why would she? She never thought to be on the lookout for people she was sleeping with being splashed across a glossy spread in a national publication.

She felt her throat tighten. Was she really that stupid? She could hear her friends all talking over each other, a mixture of exclamations and questions she didn't have the answers to. How did she not know? How could she have never happened upon this information?

Charlotte was suddenly aware that her friends were quiet. They all stared at her through the screen. Had they just asked her something? She hadn't been listening.

I can't deal with this.

Without any explanation, she ended the chat and shut her computer. She sat in silence for a few seconds, trying to process what was happening. Her phone started exploding with texts and she immediately silenced it.

In the span of two minutes, her entire life was upside down. She tried to catch her breath but couldn't inhale enough. She felt helpless. She needed more information. Information would give her control. She needed control.

She opened her computer back up and typed 'P.J. Li' into the search tab.

Images and articles popped up. She scrolled through them, literally thousands of them. She started clicking on them. Fashion magazine blogs, gossip columns, Hollywood paparazzi, basically the only kinds of articles she didn't read. There were pictures of him in his office in New York City, pictures of him opening a factory in Pennsylvania, pictures of him at fashion week in Paris...

Then came the couple photos.

'Fashion mogul P.J. Li with current flame, model Natalia Melnik.'

'French actress Camille Durand seen with American designer P.J. Li'

'Action star Mei Tao seen getting cozy with costume designer P.J. Li'

Charlotte felt herself tear up. Early in the relationship, she wondered why a good looking man like Peter had any interest in the incredibly average package she was wrapped in. Those feelings had melted away quickly when they just clicked on so many other levels, but she was still painfully aware that Peter was much better looking than she was. Seeing images of him with models and actresses...it just fit. They looked like a couple. She glanced at the framed picture on her desk. It was a selfie they had taken a month ago on a hike. She had printed that particular picture out because she loved the genuine smiles they both had, how it looked like a stock picture you'd find when you first bought the frame, the perfect lighting, and how happy they had been that day. Now, she noticed all the flaws. Her nose was too big, the bags under her eyes were prominent, her hair was greasy, she had a zit...she looked like a gargoyle stupidly smiling next to a perfect male specimen.

She wiped away tear that had finally escaped and rolled down her cheek. She exhaled loudly and felt her whole being switch gears suddenly. Why should she feel stupid? He lied to her. He lied. The entire time. He hid who he actually was from her the entire time they had been together. What else had he lied about? Did she even know who the hell he was? He hadn't even told her his name!

More tears fell and she angrily wiped them away. How dare he! He had no right to hide anything from her! She'd opened her entire life to him. She'd been nothing but honest and vulnerable. He knew everything about her and he hadn't even trusted her with his name!

She had to deal with this.

She took a deep breath and stood up. She took the walk down the hall to the spare bedroom where Peter had set up his office and she stood in the doorway. Peter was in a t shirt and pajama bottoms, leaning back in his office chair with his feet up on the desk. He had spent most of the morning in meetings, and now was rewarding himself with video games. He hadn't heard Charlotte step up before, and now she stood there, frozen, not knowing what to say. Maybe she was wrong. He didn't look like a fashion mogul. His pajama pants were frayed a little on the bottom, there was a small hole in one of his socks, and he was wearing a t shirt Charlotte had bought him last week. That's not what super rich, play boy fashion designers looked like. Maybe she was wrong. Maybe he just looked like the guy online.

There was one quick way to find out.

"Hey P.J."

There was a small explosion as Peter's thumb slipped causing his character's untimely death. He slowly put the controller down on his desk and turned himself around in his desk chair. He looked at her and she held back tears. She hadn't thought of what to say. She still hadn't decided if she was more angry at him or herself for being so oblivious. He sat quietly, hands folded while she collected herself.

"Why did you lie to me?"

"I never lied to you."

"Bullshit!" Charlotte snapped more harshly than she intended.

"It's not bullshit Charlotte. I told you exactly where I worked."

"You left out a few details."

"But I never lied."

"A lie of omission is still a lie!" Charlotte practically yelled.

Peter looked down at his hands. Charlotte took a deep breath and wiped her face. Neither one of them seemed to know what to do next. In the entire time they'd been together, they hadn't fought once. Now, every aspect of their relationship seemed false, built on a lie, and neither one of them knew what to do next. Peter readjusted in his chair, breaking the painful silence with a small squeak.

"You just..." he started quietly. "you weren't overly interested in my job, and I kind of liked that."

"You liked me being stupid?" she snapped.

"You aren't stupid and you know that's not what I meant," Peter said with a slight tinge of anger as he got up out of his chair.

"I don't know a lot about business but I know what CEO means."

"Charlotte..." Peter put his hands on his hips as he tried to think of what to say.

"Go on," Charlotte started. "But use small words so I understand."

Peter glared at her at the exact same time she scolded herself internally. She hadn't meant to sound like a moody teenager, and she hated herself for saying it. She was just so angry and her brain was trying to process the last ten minutes of her life. She should have waited. She should have slept on the information. Maybe written something out rather than barging in while she was so unstable. Or, maybe raw emotions were best. She met Peter's glare. She'd never seen him look at her that way.

Maybe raw emotions weren't best.

"Obviously you're angry. Frankly, I'm pretty pissed at the moment because my girlfriend doesn't think I know exactly how intelligent she is and I resent that."

"What exactly am I supposed to think Peter?" rational Charlotte started. "Oh I'm sorry...P.J." petulant Charlotte chimed in. "You never told me you OWNED the company you said you worked for, and just now, you told me you LIKED the fact that I wasn't smart enough to figure out who you were."

"That is not what I said."

"But it's what you meant, isn't it?"

"Of course not!" Peter's voice finally raised for the first time. "I wouldn't be with you if you were stupid."

"Then why are you with me?" she practically yelled.

"Because I love you!" he yelled back, matching her anger.

"If you loved me you would have told me the truth!"

After the sudden outbursts, the house was eerily silent. Neither of them could make eye contact with the other after a few seconds and looked down at the floor, as if the solution to the argument could be found in the carpet fibers. Charlotte silently wiped away another tear as Peter crossed and uncrossed his arms, not seeming to know what to do with the appendages. Charlotte felt the entire weight of the house on top of her. She was still trying to decide if she was mad at Peter for not telling her the whole truth, herself for not finding out on her own, or for how she handled everything that just happened.

No contest. Defiantly mad at herself for handling this fight as well as a toddler in need of a nap.

"Maybe I'll sleep at my mom's tonight. Give us both time to cool off," Peter said quietly without looking up.

"Ok," Charlotte almost whispered, her eyes never leaving the floor.

Peter stood still for another few seconds, waiting for anything else to be said. Charlotte stood against the doorway, wondering if there was anything else to say, and knowing there were paragraphs worth of things that needed to be said but nothing came. Peter took a few steps towards the door, paused briefly as they looked at each other, then softly brushed by her to grab a few things before heading off to his mother's house, leaving Charlotte alone.

2009

The excitement in the cottage was palpable.

Grandma Evelyn was as excited as Charlotte had ever seen her, which was refreshing. After Grandpa died four years ago, Grandma had seemed to age much more than her years. Not that 83 was exactly a spring chicken, but she wasn't an old lady either. She'd just been acting like an old lady the past few years and Charlotte didn't like it. It was comforting to see her up and moving with her old energy.

Uncle Matthew and Aunt Margaret were beaming and Charlotte's other Aunts and Uncles were talking over each other at a rate Charlotte was having a hard time keeping up with. Her cousins were in the other corner of the room talking, as she stood with them and listened to them talk about their lives.

Elizabeth had started a party planning business that Parker Marketing had obviously used exclusively for a few months while it got off the ground. After a few successful corporate events and two high profile wedding ceremonies, she had been able to expand the company and now had one office in New York and another in California.

Charles and William had finished at Yale and were both working in Washington DC. They were both working for a different Senator or Congressman or something. Charlotte couldn't really follow all the names they kept saying. Everyone else seemed to know who these people were so she just nodded along.

Travis had moved from modeling to music and was managing some bands that used Parker Marketing. It seemed like all he did was schedule recording sessions and photo shoots but Charlotte supposed that was pretty easy work for a 24 year old. He had an office next to Uncle Luke's and Aunt Ana seemed happy with it, so it must be going alright.

Trevor or 'Trev' as he was now known had gotten his big break into acting with a superhero movie and was plastered everywhere. Charlotte's friends had actually dragged her to the movies when 'The Legend of The Iron Fist' premiered and didn't realize she was related to the star. He'd done a nice job, but Charlotte hadn't really understood all the comic book references. She also didn't understand the posters of her cousin plastered in her friend's lockers and tried not to listen to them talk about how hot Trev Parker is. It was weird, but she didn't want anyone to know they were talking about her cousin. That would just make it extra awkward.

"They're here!" Grandma Evelyn called out as car doors could be heard closing outside. Lindsey went to the door and opened it for Benny, the new assistant Uncle Mark had brought along for the weekend, who bounded out the door to grab luggage.

A minute later, in walked George with a woman in her mid-twenties, long black hair with perfectly blown out curls, and a million dollar smile. George greeted everyone with hugs and introductions as

Charlotte's Aunts and Uncles all shook the woman's hand and talked at once.

The pair finally managed to make their way into the house from the doorway and George spoke up.

"Alright everyone, this will easier than doing this one at a time. Everyone, this is Olivia Dufort, my fiancé."

A general hurrah went up from everyone, which Charlotte thought was a little odd. It wasn't a surprise announcement. Charlotte had heard about Olivia at other family gatherings over the past three years. It was the first time she'd met her, but Charlotte was pretty sure Olivia had been at other events in New York with George. It was the first time at the cottage, which was apparently some kind of rite of passage, or final approval. Aunt Margaret had talked about it once. Apparently she and Uncle Matthew had known each other since high school, and she had been to all kinds of family functions for years, but she wasn't allowed to the cottage until they got married. She joked that she had heard so much about the cottage she at Matthew backed their wedding from December to August just so she could come. Apparently the rules had loosened a little since George and Olivia weren't married yet and here she was.

"Olivia, your father is Governor Dufort, right?" asked William.

"Proudly serving the fine people of the great state of Louisiana, yes sir," Olivia answered with a pronounced, musical accent.

"I work in Senator Rollins office. He thinks very highly of your father," Charles said.

"Well my father thinks very highly of Senator Rollins as well."

The party moved into the living room and everyone sat down, exchanging more pleasantries as Lindsey came around with wine glasses for everyone. Well, everyone but seventeen year old Charlotte of course. Charlotte listened to Olivia answer everyone's questions and fill them in on all she and George's comings and goings. She was a fascinating woman. Apparently her mother had died several years ago and she had stepped into the role of First Lady for her father when he won the Governor's race. She ran several programs through the Governor's office and Charlotte was amazed how someone so young was already so accomplished.

"Olivia dear how will your father get on without you after the wedding?" Grandma Evelyn asked after listening to Olivia tell a story of how she managed to save her father from an embarrassing gaffe with the French Ambassador.

"Well daddy won't be completely alone," Olivia started. "George and I are going to split our time between New York and Baton Rouge. Daddy just bought us the most darling little house just a few minutes from the Governor's mansion."

"Yeah I have it all worked out with Dad," George said as he looked to his father who beamed with pride. "There are a few southern clients I can take care of while I'm down there that will save them some trips up to New York. We're actually setting up an office in Baton Rouge. It won't be as big as the main office of course, just a little extension office but it'll do."

"Well enough business talk. Time for more important things," Aunt Margaret said as she sat forward and put her wine glass down. "Let's go over all the wedding plans. We only have a month to put all the final touches on everything!"

Olivia started going over all the details of the upcoming wedding. The ceremony at St. Patrick's Church, the reception at the Maison de la Luz hotel, arrivals to and from the various points in New Orleans by horse drawn carriages...Charlotte glanced at venue pictures that Olivia had brought with her and was passing around. Everything was gorgeous. She wasn't sure what she was going to wear to so many fancy places. Maybe she could wear the dress she'd worn to the junior prom last May.

Charlotte's father stepped up behind her, having gotten up to refill his wine glass.

"You looking forward to a little trip to New Orleans next month Charlie?"

"Yeah. It looks like it's going to be beautiful."

"Between your Aunt and Uncle and Governor Dufort, there is defiantly very little being left out," he said with a smirk.

"Was you and mom's wedding this fancy?"

He took a deep breath and searched his memory, as he always did when he thought about his late wife.

"This seems to be a little more over the top, but yes. Our wedding was formal and pretty fancy. It was at the Ritz, we all had limos, pictures in Central Park, the whole nine yards."

"Sounds like a lot of work."

"It was."

"Is that why you stopped seeing Jennifer? Didn't want to go through another big wedding?"

Charlotte regretted saying it as soon as it came out of her mouth. She had never really said anything while her father was dating a few years ago, and they had never talked about it when Jennifer stopped coming around. Charlotte was still fairly young when they stopped seeing each other, so she figured it just wasn't the type of thing he had wanted to discuss with his daughter. Still, she had always wondered what happened and maybe enough time had passed that he was ready to let her in.

John took a long pause, a sip of his wine, and then looked at his daughter. Charlotte had grown up quite a bit, even in the last year. She had been a bit of a late bloomer, holding on to her chubby, baby cheeks as Aunt Ana called them until last year. Now, at seventeen, she had thinned out a little, (although she wouldn't have minded thinning out a bit more) her facial features were more adult, and she carried herself with more confidence and poise than she had in the past. Her father seemed to notice that for the first time.

"If it had been right, I wouldn't have cared if she wanted a big wedding or not. There were other issues and I realized we weren't really in love. We loved the idea of each other. We were both lonely, and tried to fill the void with each other, but that's not enough. With your mom, I couldn't stand not having her around. I would miss her when she left the room. Once we got married, I couldn't remember what my life was like before I married her. I never felt that way with Jennifer. That's why I stopped seeing her."

Charlotte smiled. She had memories of her mom, but they were all from the perspective of a little girl. It was nice to hear her dad talk about her mom that way. They didn't talk about her often enough. Maybe that was something Charlotte should work on changing.

Chapter 7

Charlotte hadn't slept well.

Honestly, Charlotte hadn't slept at all.

It was an odd sensation. With the exception of a few nights here and there, that month or so with Steve last year, Charlotte had been sleeping alone for almost twenty nine years. Now suddenly, lying in bed alone made it impossible to sleep. She was currently on day three as she got up out of bed and dragged herself to the kitchen. She poured coffee grounds into the coffee maker, yawning halfway through and spilling grounds on the countertop. She let out an annoyed sigh and started the coffeemaker while she cleaned up the spill, 'cleaned' being a loose term as grounds fell to the floor and left little streaks of gritty coffee on the countertop. Normally, she would clean a spill up quickly and completely, but as she looked around at the kitchen, filled with the last few night's plates and boxes not put away, she gave up, threw the coffee grounds she had managed to sop up into the sink and rinsed off her hands. She just wanted coffee. She opened the cabinet and grabbed for her coffee mug, putting them down in front of the coffeemaker.

Both of them.

Charlotte stared down at the mugs. She hadn't meant to grab two.

She stared at the mugs as the pot finished brewing and finally, exhaustion and depression took over.

Charlotte let everything out and sobbed, sinking down to the floor with her back against the cabinet. She'd spent the last three days going back and forth between so lonely and depressed she could barely get out of bed to being so angry at Peter for lying to her she wanted to scream. She wasn't sure which Charlotte was sobbing her eyes out on the spilled coffee grounds on her kitchen floor, but she didn't care. She just knew she was miserable.

Charlotte wiped her eyes and put her head back against the cabinet. She couldn't keep going like this. She hadn't answered her phone for three days, aside from her father, and she hadn't mentioned anything about the fight to him. He loved Peter and Charlotte didn't want to upset him. Janice, Hannah, and Katie had all called and Charlotte had about fifty unread texts from them but she didn't know what to tell them. She didn't know what to tell her father.

She had to figure something out.

She picked herself up with determination and took a shower, put on the first clean clothes she pulled out of the drawer and grabbed her purse without even drying her hair. Normally, Charlotte would use driving as an opportunity to plan and organize her thoughts, but this morning, there was nothing but blind determination.

She pulled up to Mrs. Li's house, parked quickly on the street and marched up to the door. It wasn't until after she knocked that she realized she had no idea what she wanted to say. This was also when she realized it was six in the morning. Maybe no one was awake yet. Charlotte's determination started waning and she started to turn to go back home.

The door opened and she was greeted by the face she'd been missing, holding his coffee cup, the same pajama bottoms he'd been wearing the night he left. He had a little stubble which Charlotte had never seen. He was always clean shaven, even when he looked a little disheveled. They stood in silence for a few beats and Charlotte was suddenly very aware of her wet hair, yoga pants, and oversized hoodie. Even so, she may have been more put together than Peter was for the first time.

"Charlotte Parker," he said quietly.

She met his gaze and her voice cracked a little.

"Peter Li."

He looked over at the small chairs on the corner of the wrap around porch.

"You want to have a seat? Maybe we can talk."

Charlotte nodded.

"Ok. Let me just put my cup down."

Charlotte took a seat as Peter put his coffee mug down in the kitchen. Charlotte sat nervously, trying to formulate what exactly she wanted to say and coming up empty. She was still swinging back and forth between anger and sadness, but all she knew was she wanted to talk about it, and Peter was the only one she wanted to talk to. She fidgeted awkwardly in the chair, waiting for Peter to come back. He seemed to be taking a ridiculous amount of time, but when he finally reappeared, he was wearing a hoodie. He must have run up to his room.

"Little chilly this morning," he said as he sat down next to her.

Charlotte nodded. "Little chilly the past few days." She said quietly.

Peter nodded.

They sat in silence for a minute, awkwardly looking from the deck, to each other, to the street, then back to the deck. Finally Charlotte sat up and broke the silence.

"I'm so sorry for how I reacted," she started. Peter looked up at her, having settled on folded hands in front of him with his forearms on his thighs.

"It was childish, and ridiculous, and disrespectful, and it wasn't what you deserved Peter."

"Wasn't it?" he asked. Charlotte furrowed her brow. He sighed, looked back down at the deck, then started again.

"I did lie to you. That was childish, and ridiculous and incredibly disrespectful. You don't lie to the people you love."

"You shouldn't yell at the people you love either," Charlotte said, guilt overtaking her. "You didn't deserve to be yelled at."

"Maybe not," Peter smiled slightly. "But the anger was justified."

He looked at her, taking a moment to really look over her entire face. Charlotte ran a self-conscience hand through her damp hair.

"I am so sorry I lied to you Charlotte. I was just enjoying things as they were and I didn't want anything to change it."

"I get that. I suppose things would have been different if I'd known. I mean, I hope they wouldn't have, but there's no way it would have been as...I guess normal is the right word."

"It is the right word," Peter said as he sat back. "I live in a very weird world. I didn't really understand that until I hit thirty. I was dating an actress, and literally flying out to California every week or two, and it finally just hit me...that wasn't normal. I didn't even like her that much. Her agent set us up because it got her picture taken more if she was dating someone. I realized I was flying across the country supposedly to see my girlfriend, but I was more excited about a business deal I was going to make while I was out there. That wasn't the life I wanted."

"I suppose that makes sense," Charlotte said, memories of the big windows overlooking Central Park, the town cars with uniformed drivers, and gold trimmed everything flooding her mind. "I remember living like that with my parents in the city. It was a little much, wasn't it?"

He nodded in agreement. "I used to live in this ridiculous place. Two stories, big open rooms with modern furniture and expensive high end everything. When I got back from that trip to California that I was just telling you about, I sold it and moved into a new place. I have a nice apartment in New York. It's defiantly nicer than a lot of places, but it's not opulent. It's not over the top. It's just a nice place in a building with families and retired people and it's all I need."

Charlotte looked down at her yoga pants. It was nice to hear him say he didn't need anything fancy considering what she looked like at the moment.

"So, is that where I fit in?" she asked. "I'm normal?"

"No. You're extraordinary."

She rolled her eyes.

"I thought you weren't going to lie to me."

"I'm not lying."

"Peter," She stopped and collected herself. She finally realized why she had been so upset. She understood why she hadn't been able to put her finger on it and it suddenly became crystal clear. It was so obvious now she internally chastised herself for not figuring it out sooner. She could have saved herself several days of exhaustion if she'd managed to piece this together.

"Before I knew who you are," Charlotte started, "we made sense. You were just some guy who worked in sales for a company. You were going to be able to move here and find a job in Burlington or something here in town even. We'd just be a normal little family, but now..." she looked down at the porch. "Now we can't be normal. You run a huge company in New York so we can't have a normal life here. I don't understand us now."

"What's not to understand?" Peter asked honestly.

She gave an exasperated sigh.

"Why me?"

"I love you."

"You dated models and actresses."

"And broke up with them because they were vapid and shallow."

"Also really good looking and rich."

"So?"

"I just..." Charlotte stopped. "Peter I don't measure up."

Peter smiled.

"Charlotte, you are so beyond my ex-girlfriends you can't be measured on the same scale. You might not think you're beautiful, but I do. You're kind, you're honest, you are much, much smarter than I am."

"Don't patronize me Mr. Millionaire," Charlotte laughed.

"Money and brains don't always go together. Yes, I'm smart, but I also got unbelievably lucky and had a great support system behind me. And now I have you as part of my support system so I have a feeling I'm going to be unstoppable. And I disagree with you about being normal. Lots of normal people live in New York. We can find a normal life in New York."

Charlotte laughed as Peter sat back and pulled something out of the pocket on the front of his hoodie.

"I was so glad you came over today because I bought you something yesterday. I was planning on coming back home tonight, but I don't want to wait, so I really hope you don't mind the sweats and hoodie."

Charlotte looked at him and froze as he situated himself on one knee.

"The last few days have been unbearable because you weren't in them. I don't want another day like that. I want you to be my support and I want to be yours."

He opened the box and Charlotte gasped audibly.

"Charlotte Parker, will you marry me?"

Charlotte gasped again, feeling light headed from the lack of oxygen, and trying to slow her heart rate enough so she could breathe. She let out a small cry, covering her mouth with her hands before smiling so big her face hurt. She tucked a half dry piece of hair behind her ear, and managed to gasp out

"Yes."

Peter smiled and dropped his other knee, coming in close to her and kissing her deeply as she threw her arms around his neck. He wrapped his arms around her, and they felt all the weight of the past few days melt away. Everything suddenly made sense again. When they finally managed to decouple and back a few inches away from each other, Peter took the ring out of the box and Charlotte held out a shaking left hand. As he put the ring on her finger, Charlotte couldn't help but think this was the most abnormal, but somehow normal moment of her life.

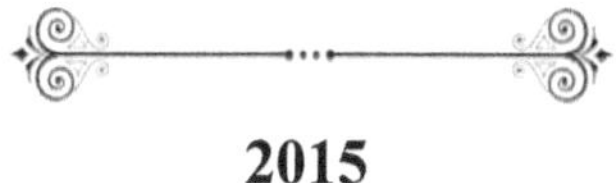

2015

Charlotte escaped to the back porch and took a breath.

The cottage was packed to the brim and she just needed a quiet moment before dinner. She took a few slow steps over to the rocking chairs on the porch and took a seat. She sat back, took a sip of wine, and let herself rock slightly and enjoy the relative quiet.

Over the past few years, Charlotte had seen more of her extended family than she had during her entire childhood, and after two full days in the cottage with everyone, she just needed a break.

It had started back in 2009 with George and Olivia's wedding in Louisiana. Charlotte remembered feeling silly getting into her prom dress from a few months before to go to the wedding, but quickly realized she was almost underdressed when she had arrived. She had felt like royalty riding around New Orleans in a horse drawn carriage, eating little pastries at the reception, and her dad letting her have a few sips of champagne during the toasts.

Of course the royal feeling was nothing compared to Elizabeth's wedding in 2010. She had married Ian who was some kind of title Charlotte still didn't understand. He wasn't a Prince, but when they all trooped out to England for their wedding, they got a tour of his family's estate and he certainly seemed like a Prince or a Duke or something. It was the first time (and Charlotte hoped the last time) she ever had to have a hat pinned into her hair. Whoever came up with that painful tradition needed to be shot.

William's wedding had been next and seemed like a quiet, small affair by comparison to Elizabeth's, but was still gorgeous. His wife Bella's family owned a couple hotels in New York and they got married in a rooftop ceremony, which Grandma had opposed in the strongest of terms, but finally agreed it would have been strange for Bella to get married in the Episcopal church since she was Jewish. Charlotte had really enjoyed the big band at the reception and how the city looked at night from the rooftop. It was the first time she had really seen the city lit up at night from that vantage point and it really was magical.

In 2013, there had been 'that awful woman' at Charles and Rebecca's wedding, but you couldn't really blame her. You can't really help when you go into labor, and Travis didn't exactly help the situation. His girlfriend Savannah went into labor during the reception, and Travis wasn't able to drive her to the hospital, seeing as he was drunk off his ass. Charlotte secretly wondered if she had named their daughter 'Koi' as some kind of payback since she ended up giving birth alone at the hospital and Travis hated the name.

Then Trevor's classic Hollywood wedding, which Elizabeth's firm had planned and had apparently cost over $1.5 million if the tabloids were to be believed. His wife, actress Taylor Rose, had met him during filming and every aspect of their relationship had been well documented. Charlotte had spent most of that wedding hiding from cameras and wasn't sure there was any tangible proof she had been in attendance.

With all of her cousins married, she thought things were going to quiet down, but as most married couples do, they all started procreating and the cottage was currently overstuffed with children, nannies, and relatives drinking, talking, and laughing. Charlotte wasn't overly comfortable around kids to begin with, and there was quite a troop in the cottage:

There were George and Olivia's children, four year old Michael and one year old Sarah.

Elizabeth and Ian's daughter, three year old Catherine.

Charles and Rebecca's son Robert, making his first cottage appearance at five months.

William and Bella's one year old, Philip.

And of course, Travis and Savannah's two year old daughter Koi.

Six kids under five years old. Charlotte took another solid sip of her wine just thinking about it.

A door on the other side of the porch opened and Charlotte looked over. Lindsey came out talking on her cell phone. Charlotte didn't think she had ever seen Lindsey on her cell phone at the cottage. She was usually so busy setting things up and cooking for everyone she barely had time to sit down, let alone take a phone call.

"...and what did the doctor say?"

Oh this is not a good conversation.

"I'm at work out of town. I don't know..."

Oh this is not a good conversation at all.

Charlotte got up and walked over to Lindsey who was holding back tears on the phone. Charlotte didn't want to interrupt what was obviously a private moment, but something wasn't right.

"Lindsey?"

"Oh Charlotte. I'm so sorry I didn't see you there."

"No worries, its fine. What's wrong?"

"My mom fell. She's in an assisted living home and she fell. The nurses don't know how bad it is and I don't know what to do."

"Have Benny drive you back to the city in one of the town cars. I'm sure Grandma will understand."

"But dinner's on and this is the big weekend..."

"Lindsey. Go. I'll take care of it."

A relieved smile crossed Lindsey's face as she told the person on the phone she was on her way. She went back to the annex house to grab her luggage and Charlotte found Benny and let him know what was going on. She waved good bye to Benny and Lindsey as they drove off and then went in to the kitchen, suddenly realizing she had no clue what Lindsey had been cooking. Something smelled good, so she peeked in the oven and saw something...a roast maybe?...and various vegetables in different states of preparation on the countertop. Figuring she couldn't screw up veggies too badly, she started cooking, and managed to pull together a dish of asparagus, some mashed potatoes, and she threw together a salad. As she tasted things, she decided it wasn't as good as Lindsey's cooking, but it probably wasn't going to kill anyone, so she started setting things out on the table. She pulled the roast out and started cutting slices of maybe slightly over cooked meat, but better over than under, right?

She got everything set out on the table and called everyone over, grabbing another bottle of wine and refilling glasses as everyone sat down.

"Why the table side service Charlotte? Are you putting that history degree of yours to work?" Aunt Julia teased as Charlotte refilled her wine glass.

"No. Lindsey had a family emergency so I told her to go and I just jumped in to finish up. I hope that was ok Grandma."

"Of course dear," Grandma Evelyn said with genuine concern. "I do hope everything is alright."

"Her mom fell at the assisted living home and had to be taken to the hospital. I asked Benny to drive her back to the city and then bring the car back tomorrow morning. I didn't want him driving back out here that late."

"Very good thinking dear," Grandma said as the table turned their attention to the meal.

Everyone ate and gossiped about goings on in the city. The nannies at the children's table quietly cleaned spills and Rebecca got up to hold Robert and feed him when he started fussing. Charlotte watched everyone eat and quietly congratulated herself. She wasn't a great cook by any stretch of the imagination but everyone seemed to be enjoying things, so she was counting this as a big win. Every so often she'd pop up to refill a wine glass or take a serving plate back to the kitchen. *Asparagus went fast! They really must've liked that one!*

As everyone finished, they congregated back in the living room, playing with the children and still gossiping about what was going on in the city, Charlotte cleared the table and filled the dishwasher, satisfied with a job well done.

She finished cleaning the kitchen and poured herself a glass of wine before sitting down at the now cleared table with her laptop. She had some work she needed to get done this weekend on her Master's thesis and she hadn't gotten as far as she had hoped. Now that the kids were being put to bed upstairs and things had quieted down, she figured she could get some work done. A few card games had broken out and she figured no one would bother her while she made a few edits and filled in a few citations she had written out but hadn't added to the paper yet. Her cousin Elizabeth had the same idea and had situated herself at a kitchen chair with her laptop, obviously working on something.

A computer duet started playing as they both quietly typed away, broken only by an occasional sip of wine or Charlotte crossing something off in her notebook as she got it entered on her computer.

"Charlotte."

Elizabeth broke Charlotte out of her rhythm and she looked up.

"I'm working here, and I really need to concentrate."

Charlotte looked at her work space and wondered what the distraction was.

"I'm sorry. I didn't realize I was bothering you," Charlotte said sincerely, not meaning to have distracted her cousin. Elizabeth had always been a very serious worker, and worked throughout the reunions, always seeming to be on her phone or laptop. She and Aunt Julia were actually very similar in that regard.

"Well I'm working on something really important, so if you could play your game or whatever somewhere else, I'd really appreciate it." Elizabeth turned her attention back to her laptop and continued typing.

"I'm not playing a game. I'm working on my Master's degree."

"Ok well this is really important and I need to focus," Elizabeth said without looking up. Charlotte sat still for a moment, stunned. She was just sitting and working quietly...how was she distracting anyone? Her Aunts, Uncles, and cousins were all in the room, drinking, playing games and talking. It wasn't as if this was a quiet little corner. The noise level had gone down considerably since the children had been carted off to bed, but the room was still filled and the dining room table was essentially in the middle of the hub.

Still, Charlotte could do this work anywhere. It was just transferring information from her notebook to her computer. She could work anywhere. She put her notebook on top of her keyboard and took her wine glass to the back porch. It was a nice night...this was better she told herself.

Charlotte transferred a few more citations and quietly got in a groove when she heard the door open. She glanced up and smiled at her grandmother as she came out and sat down next to her.

"Wonderful to have the house so full, isn't it dear?"

Charlotte nodded, not really agreeing but understanding why this all made her grandmother so happy. Grandma Evelyn had always been the center of the family solar system, and she just radiated everything you would want in the leader of the family. Nothing made her happier than when the family was all together, and as her grandchildren had grown up, they'd started forging their own paths, so Charlotte knew it made her incredibly happy to have everyone under the same roof.

"Maybe next year the house will be a little more full?" her grandmother asked looking at Charlotte with a sideways glance and a smile. Charlotte knew what she was saying but decided to play a little.

"Do you think Elizabeth and Ian are going to have another baby?"

"Possibly, but that's not what I was saying."

"I'm a little busy with my Master's right now. Maybe in a few years," Charlotte said, laughing it off and turning back to her computer.

"You need to get out there. I know several young men in New York that would be perfect for you."

"Grandma, I don't live in New York."

"You could come stay with me for a bit. I'm sure Matthew can get you a job at the firm."

"Lots of job openings in the history department of a marketing firm?"

"Oh dear it doesn't matter. You have a degree and the Parker name. You're a clever girl and I'm sure Matthew could find a good place for you."

Charlotte suddenly realized her grandmother wasn't joking.

"Grandma, that's really nice, but I'm not really interested in working in marketing."

"Well what are you planning to do dear?"

"I'm not sure...Maybe teaching, maybe working for a museum or a national monument...I'm just enjoying school right now."

"Well that's all well and good, but I'm worried about you. I don't want you to end up alone."

"Grandma, I'm only 23. I'm not exactly an old maid."

"When's the last time you dated anyone?"

What is happening right now?

"Grandma, I'm fine, really."

"I know you are dear," she said as she patted Charlotte's knee and sat back in her chair. Charlotte laughed a little internally and wondered if all her cousins had gotten this same level of interest in their personal lives. Maybe her Uncles had. She laughed a little thinking about her father at her age getting this talking to. She was suddenly very glad her father didn't seem overly interested in her dating history. (a short history to be sure, but it was there...kind of.)

They sat quietly for another few minutes while Charlotte worked on her laptop before Grandma started again.

"You know the Hillers, right? Their granddaughter is back in New York now. She just finished her degree at UCLA."

"That's nice," Charlotte said, confused at the topic change.

"I think the two of you would really hit it off."

"Grandma, I'm not gay."

"I just want you to be happy dear."

Charlotte took another big sip of wine and laughed.

"Well I'm glad you are looking out for me, but I swear, I'm fine. I'm just focused on school right now."

"Alright dear," her grandmother said, somewhat resigned. "I just want you to focus on yourself too. There's more to life than school or work. I want you to be happy with your life."

"I will be grandma."

That seemed to satisfy her grandmother, who got up and went back in the house. Charlotte smiled and shook her head a little, hoping she believed what she had just told her grandmother. The idea of bringing someone new here, introducing him to everyone...she hadn't really thought about it until now. It seemed like a foreign concept. She was only 23...she shouldn't be thinking about marriage and kids yet, right? Still, her cousins weren't that much older than she was, and they were all getting married and having kids. Her parents had been in their mid-20's when they got married. Her mom was 26 when Charlotte was born. That was only three years away. Was Charlotte falling behind? Should she be actively searching for Mr. Right? Or apparently Miss Right as far as her grandmother seemed to be concerned.

One of the younger children let out a wail from inside. Apparently bedtime wasn't going so well. One wailing child quickly lead to three as they all fed off each other.

Maybe being single wasn't actually such a bad thing.

Yeah, defiantly not something she would ever rush into.

Chapter 8

Peter hadn't been kidding. His apartment in New York was nice.

She adjusted her mask as she told the movers where to put the furniture she had decided to bring with her and smiled as things started taking shape. She and Peter had spent the week after their engagement turning their lives upside down, going to New York and getting Peter's apartment ready to be Peter and Charlotte's apartment. This unfortunately included airing the place out after Peter realized he hadn't cleaned out his refrigerator before living in Vermont for five months. Fortunately, he had been enough of a stereotypical single man that there wasn't much food left in the kitchen to spoil, and they were able to get rid of the smell within a week. The apartment was also rather sparse, so she was able to move a pretty good amount of her things in and really make the place homey.

Peter had gone to his office for a few in person meetings, something New York was just starting to do again as the COVID-19 pandemic had shut the city down for months, but he was starting to do a few things at the office as she stayed behind and set up the household.

Charlotte had also made the painful choice to resign her position at the library. She knew it had to happen as soon as she agreed to move to New York, but there was still such a finality to it. But Peter had come up with a great idea that Charlotte was equal parts excited and nervous about. He suggested she jump in to a doctoral program and she agreed it was the perfect time. She'd been kicking the idea around but didn't see the point of spending all the money on getting a doctorate with no plan beyond continuing to work at the library. Now, Peter said, she had all of New York City to look for a job. All the museums, all the universities, and he jokingly pointed out, he had a little money saved up and could help her out.

After the movers left, Charlotte took off her mask and started looking around at all the boxes. She should start unpacking and putting everything away, but the task was a little overwhelming.

Maybe just the kitchen. Just one room and then you can make a nice dinner tonight.

Charlotte fired up the Hamilton soundtrack on her phone and started ripping open boxes in the kitchen. Peter had his own dishes and cookware but had freely admitted he only had enough plates for himself and only two pots. Charlotte added all of her kitchenware to the kitchen and by the end of the Hamilton soundtrack, the kitchen, dining table, and cupboard she had brought from her house were all fully stocked and ready for proper meals. She broke down the boxes and decided since she was going downstairs with them, she might as well use the opportunity to explore her new surroundings. She grabbed her purse and mask (still the strangest thing to adapt to under the circumstances) and brought the deconstructed boxes down to the basement before heading out to the street. A quick google search told her where Peter's office was.

Wow. A fifteen minute walk. He wasn't kidding when he said short commute.

Charlotte headed off in the direction of the office building, taking in the sites of the city as she went. It was very different than what she was used to. Within five minutes, she'd passed at least fifty people. There were cars lined up on the street bumper to bumper, and more ambient noise than she had ever heard in as long as she could remember. Still, it was homey and comfortable, and while she was very overwhelmed with everything, she felt like she could feel at home here.

The buildings started taking on a more business like feeling and she found the right building right as Google told her she had arrived. There were people moving around the building, but she could tell it was only a fraction of the normal volume. That made it easier to check the directory and she enjoyed a quiet elevator ride up to the 22nd floor. The elevator let her off to a beautifully decorated lobby with the Thunderbolt logo behind the reception desk. A young man sat behind a plexiglass shield and wearing a mask with the Thunderbolt logo on it. He greeted her with what Charlotte was sure was a smile.

"How can I help you?"

"I'm here to see Peter. Li," she added awkwardly, realizing there could be more than one Peter working here.

"Do you have an appointment?"

Charlotte was taken aback slightly. It hadn't even occurred to her that Peter didn't have the sort of job where she could just drop in. She hadn't thought to make an appointment or even ask Peter if she could drop by for lunch. Just one more thing to get used to in this new normal.

"Um, no. I didn't think to make an appointment, sorry. Is he available?"

The young man looked at his computer and back at her a little more quickly than Charlotte thought it was possible to get the information.

"No I'm sorry. Mr. Li is in back to back meetings today. If you leave your name and business I can see if we can get you scheduled in next week."

"No that's ok."

Charlotte turned to go.

Wait a minute. This is stupid!

She pulled her phone out of her purse and sent Peter a text.

"Hey. I'm in your lobby. You want to sneak away for lunch?"

She hit send and put her phone away, looking back at the man at the desk with a smug smile under her mask. Within thirty seconds, the phone on the young man's desk rang and he answered it.

"Yes sir?...Yes...Of course sir."

He hung up and looked at Charlotte.

"If you'll come with me I'll take you to Mr. Li's office."

"Thank you."

The young man lead Charlotte through the office. It was a pleasant looking place, but only a few people were sitting at the mostly empty desks. Peter had said most of his employees were still working at home and the 'return to work' policies were taking up most of his week, dealing with giving employees more flexible schedules, work at home support, and doing some restructuring that he was confident would mean he wouldn't have to fire anyone. Peter said that overall, Thunderbolt hadn't suffered too much during the pandemic, but, it wasn't over yet so he was working overtime to make sure things stayed stable enough for his employees. He'd had a few rough days over the past few months, but generally speaking, he had told Charlotte they were going to be ok.

The young man brought Charlotte back to another desk outside a door and looked at the young woman at the desk.

"This is Miss Parker for Mr. Li."

The woman nodded and gestured to the door.

"You can head in Miss Parker."

Charlotte thanked both of them and opened the door to the office. Peter was at his desk, in between two big beautiful banks of windows looking out through the city. It was a little bit nicer than the view she had had from her office in the library in Vermont for sure.

"Charlotte Parker. This is a surprise," he said as he got up from his desk and the two of them took their masks off to share a kiss.

"I thought you might like to sneak away for lunch."

"I'm booked solid, I don't know if Greg told you."

"He did. I guess I was hoping he was just trying to get rid of me because I didn't have an appointment."

"Oh. Sorry about that. I'll make sure Greg and Valerie put you on the walk in list."

"Ooooo...the walk in list," Charlotte teased. "What did I do to deserve this high honor?"

"You sleep with me, so that was what really put you over the top."

"Is that how Greg got on the walk in list?"

"Yeah but he broke my heart so Val had to take him off."

Charlotte laughed. "Ok. Well if you're really busy I won't bother you for lunch."

"No, stay. I was just going to order in to the office in a minute here and I'd love the company. Especially since it's you. We can make it a working lunch."

"Working lunch?"

"Yes. I have a proposal for you."

"Another one? I really liked the last one."

"Well I hope you like this one too." He said as he picked up the phone. "Caesar salad ok?"

"Great."

He put the phone to his ear and tapped a button.

"Val can you send in a couple Caesar salads in for Charlotte and I?... Thanks."

He gestured to the oversized chairs and they took a seat.

"So, I thought we should talk about wedding plans."

"Yeah. Weddings in the time of COVID are an interesting topic, aren't they?"

Ever since the pandemic had hit, large gatherings were basically a no go. Anything that brought large groups of people together in enclosed spaces was a sure way to get people sick, so weddings all over the world had been postponed. Charlotte had been so excited after the proposal and so busy organizing her life the past two weeks moving to New York she hadn't really put much thought into the wedding.

The door opened and Valerie walked in with a tray filled with two bowls, two bottles of water, and some silverware. She put it down on the table between Peter and Charlotte and stepped back.

"Anything else Mr. Li?

"Thanks Val, this is great. One thing...this is Charlotte Parker. Can you make sure she's on the walk in please?"

"Absolutely."

She turned and left and Charlotte laughed.

"I can't get over the big office and the walk in list and people calling you Mr. Li. I thought you swore to me you were normal."

"Hey I confessed everything and you still said yes so you're stuck with me now."

"Yeah ok," Charlotte laughed as she picked up her bowl and started mixing her salad. "So let's talk wedding. What did you have in mind?"

Peter finished chewing his first bite of salad and started slowly. Peter had a way of absolutely switching character depending on the topic. Most of the time, he was relaxed, had that million dollar smile she loved so much, and was in to the same nerdy, silly things that she was. But then, he could morph into an almost entirely different person when there was a serious topic on the table. Charlotte felt herself get nervous for a split second, scared he was about to drop some kind of major bombshell on her.

"The number one thing I want to do is give you whatever kind of wedding you want. Based on the family you come from, I'm imagining weddings are big deals."

"Little bit," Charlotte said as she thought back over all the weddings she'd been to over the last decade. She suddenly felt very self-conscious. She had been so excited to marry Peter that she hadn't really thought about what that meant. Four hundred people watching her walk down the aisle of a grandiose church, then everyone watching her dance with Peter in a huge ballroom. Why did little girls dream of that? It was basically her worst nightmare.

"So that's my concern," Peter said breaking her out of her wedding nightmare. "Obviously, we can't do that right now. I hate the idea of waiting a year or more until COVID is under control to marry you. What would you think about a small legal ceremony in Vermont, then we could do something big for one of our anniversaries if you want. Whenever this thing is under control. It's just an idea and if you hate it, that's fine. We can wait and do whatever you want in a year or two if that's what you want. It was just an idea but under the current world circumstances, I just thought it would be a good plan to do it..."

"Next Tuesday," Charlotte interrupted.

Peter stared at her in stunned silence. "What?"

"Next Tuesday. It's perfect. September first. We can get our license this week and do it at the courthouse next Tuesday. We could have a little lunch after at your mom's house, Janice could take pictures, your mom has those great trees in her backyard so it'll be beautiful. Next Tuesday."

Peter sat in silence, a piece of salad hanging off his fork because he had forgotten he was eating lunch. It was usually Peter who took Charlotte completely off guard, so neither one of them knew how to deal with the sudden role reversal. In Charlotte's mind, it made perfect sense. A quiet ceremony where only her closest friends and family would be looking at her, but there was a perfectly valid reason and no one could give her a hard time about not doing something big. It was perfect.

She looked at Peter and smiled. He smiled back.

"It's a date."

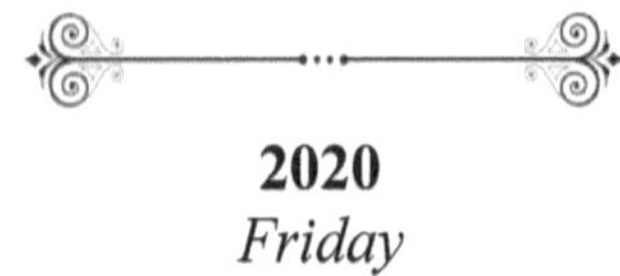

2020
Friday

"Another ten miles, then you take a right," Charlotte said as Peter turned onto the back country road Charlotte knew so well. She hadn't come this way to the cottage since she was a child, but this was the same road she and her father used to take from the opposite direction, so she still felt like she knew it. She put her phone down and turned her attention back to the photo album she had on her lap.

Janice had taken beautiful pictures. She even had all the pictures printed out and put them in the photo book, then drove down to New York to deliver it so Charlotte and Peter had wedding pictures to show off at the reunion.

Judge Miller, a friend of her father's, had agreed to officiate and had asked his daughter (who worked at city hall) to get the marriage license ready. Peter and Charlotte had returned to the same store Peter purchased her engagement ring and by a small miracle, found wedding bands that fit both of them. Not that it would have been the end of the world to wait a few extra days after the ceremony to have wedding bands, but it was a nice detail to actually be able to exchange rings on their actual wedding day rather than waiting for them to be resized.

Charlotte had found an adorable white sundress and a headband with some crystal detail at Katie's store, and Peter 'really dressed to impress' as he said, wearing the one suit with a vest he owned, but ended up ditching the jacket five minutes before the ceremony after he caught his arm on a loose nail and ripped the elbow to shreds. It was so hot, Peter was happy to ditch the jacket and roll his shirt sleeves up. Charlotte thought the shirt and vest without the jacket looked better anyway, so, happy accident.

Peter's friend Tom brought their wedding cake, in the form of a giant cookie with dozens of other cookies that he set up with frosting and other toppings, and the entire wedding party had an impromptu cookie decorating contest. Charlotte thought Janice won, but everyone was nice enough to give the honorary prize to the newlyweds.

Mrs. Li had done a beautiful job with her backyard, decorating with flowers and a tall garden arch for the ceremony. Janice took pictures like a pro, posing Peter and Charlotte into the most adorable positions that somehow managed to look totally natural instead of staged, not to mention the perfectly timed candids she took. Hannah brought her bluetooth speakers and made a ceremony and reception playlist and everyone had stayed for hours longer than Charlotte thought they would. Charlotte particularly liked the pictures of Mrs. Li and her father dancing. They had gotten to be very good friends over the last few months, and it really showed in the pictures. Peter's mom acted as the cater as well as venue hostess and had made enough food to feed the entire town. She even came prepared with to go boxes and sent the guests home with leftovers to last a week.

They spent their wedding night at Charlotte's house, which was basically devoid of furniture, with the exception of a mattress on the floor, a card table that the realtor had set up in the living room with the listing information, and the overnight bags they had brought with them from New York. They spent the next morning watching videos on Charlotte's phone while writing thank you cards at the card table, before heading back to New York for the rest of their staycation honeymoon. They'd agreed they would take an actual trip for their one year anniversary. Maybe London.

"So how well do I need to behave myself?" Peter joked. "I'm not allowed to cuss at all, right?" Charlotte laughed at that. She was the cusser in their house, although she had noted Peter had started taking after her a little in the past month or so.

"Just not around my grandmother."

At 94, Grandma Evelyn was still the ruler of the family. She was a healthy 94 but spent most of her time at the latest reunions sitting in one of the comfy chairs of the cottage. She had a wheelchair which she had fought fiercely but had finally agreed to use when Lindsey reminded her of her own mother's fall a few years back that had eventually led to hip surgery that had never healed properly.

"You said she's really religious, right?"

"She had four boys and named them Matthew, Mark, Luke, and John."

"Ok so REALLY religious."

"Little bit. Uncle Matthew and Aunt Margaret are too, and Uncle Mark. Aunt Julia plays along but I don't know how serious she is about it. Uncle Luke couldn't care less."

"What about your cousins?"

"George is pretty religious, and I think Charles and William are, but I'm not really sure," she looked at her husband and smiled. "Don't worry. I doubt they'll kick us heathens out of the house."

"I'm just hoping I don't get struck by lightning on Sunday."

Charlotte laughed as Peter slowed the car down and turned onto the familiar driveway. Charlotte slipped her shoes on and put the photo album back in her bag with her laptop and all the application paperwork she was working on for her doctoral program applications. She had decided on a few different programs to apply for and wanted to get a jump start on all the applications this weekend so she could start in January. She had kind of scoffed at the idea when Peter suggested it, but the thought of teaching at NYU or working in one of the museums had gotten her really excited. It was something she'd always had in the back of her mind, but she never thought it was achievable. Of course, six months ago she wouldn't have thought she would be bringing her husband of four days to the cottage to meet her entire family, so who knew what twists and turns were ahead of her.

Peter parked the car next to the line of black town cars and popped the keys in his pocket. He turned to Charlotte and she smiled.

"You ready to meet them, Peter Li?"

He smiled back, that same soft smile she'd fallen for just a few short months ago.

"Let's go, Charlotte Parker-Li."

They shared a quick kiss and got out of the car as Benny came out the door and toward the car to grab bags. Lindsey had wheeled Grandma out to the porch and Charlotte could see her beaming smile all the way from there. The sheer gravitational pull of Grandma Evelyn drew the newlyweds up to the porch and Charlotte bent down and gave her a gentle hug and kiss as soon as she hit the top stair.

"Grandma, let me introduce you to my husband, Peter Li."

Peter smiled and held out his hand, but Grandma was having none of that. With a quick jerk that surprised Peter, she grabbed his hand and yanked him in for a hug and kiss on the cheek.

"Welcome to the family Peter."

"Thank you," he said with a laugh and a smile, still recovering from his new grandmother's surprising strength. He extended a hand to Lindsey. "And you are?"

"Lindsey, sir," she said shaking his hand. "I'm Mrs. Parker's cook and housekeeper."

"Very nice to meet you Lindsey."

Peter and Charlotte followed them in as Peter got his first look at the cottage Charlotte had described to him so many times. His eyes went immediately up to the high roofline and the triangle windows at the peak of the living room. He stopped and admired the windows for a minute while Charlotte took a few steps ahead and then turned around. She stopped and turned back to him, giving him an inquisitive look. He silently motioned to the windows, the sharp edges juxtaposed against the fluffy, white clouds and the softly dimming sky in the evening light. She looked up and smiled, seeing the inspiration for the painting that hung in her mother in law's house with new appreciation. She felt Peter step up behind her and put his arm around her waist, giving her a little peck on the forehead before they continued into the house.

"It's so nice out, everyone went down to the fire pit for cocktail hour. I was going to head down myself but wanted to wait for you."

"Thanks Grandma," Charlotte said as she put her purse and bag down on the stairs and then headed toward the back porch. Peter quietly took Charlotte's hand and they followed Lindsey out to the back porch and met her and Grandma Evelyn at the bottom of the ramp they had had installed two years ago when the wheelchair became needed.

They took a slow stroll down to the fire pit, keeping pace with Lindsey as she wheeled Grandma Evelyn on the neat stone path. As they got close, they could hear laughs and conversation, that were suddenly silenced when Charlotte's father stood up and loudly announced their arrival. The entire Parker tribe got up almost in unison and descended on the newlyweds. Charlotte inhaled sharply, slightly overwhelmed with the attention, and Peter squeezed her hand gently and braced himself for the onslaught. He shook hands and greeted his new family, got pulled in for hugs from his new Aunts, and greeted everyone with a genuine smile. Charlotte was amazed. Being an only child herself, but with a large extended family, she was used to both being alone and surrounded by family. Peter didn't have an extended family, but he easily fit into the role, or at least acted like it was natural for him. Charlotte wondered if his natural way with a group of unknown people was one of the reasons Thunderbolt was as successful as it was.

After what seemed to Charlotte like an hour of introductions, everyone resettled in their seats and Lindsey started handing around glasses of champagne and Grandma Evelyn lead a toast to the newest addition to the Parker clan.

"So Peter," Aunt Julia started. "I never would have thought in a million years I would be seeing you here after the last time we met."

"I'm sorry, last time?" Peter started before the memory came back to him. "Wait, Julia Parker, yes. We met a few years back about Thunderbolt using Parker marketing." Everyone nodded and laughed slightly, and Peter turned a slight shade of red.

"I hope I'm not about to be kicked out of the family four days in?"

"Of course not darling." Julia said. "Not getting the Thunderbolt account was the kick I needed to step back and just stay on the board of directors. Leave the client wooing to the younger folk."

"Which reminds me," William interjected. "I'd love to sit down with you and talk about your marketing needs."

Everyone laughed and Peter politely waved it off through a smile.

"We're pretty happy with our in house marketing people, thanks."

Obviously looking to change the subject, Peter looked at George.

"You're Congressman, Parker, right?"

"Yes sir," George said with his adopted Louisiana drawl he adopted when he ran for Congress two years before. Charlotte had laughed out loud the first time she saw her cousin on TV and heard his voice. She'd never heard him with anything than his slight New York accent, and she remembered him talking about working with a dialect coach so he could seem more like a Louisiana native to the voters. Charlotte had thought he should ask for his money back.

"That's quite an accomplishment," Peter said politely. Charlotte had told Peter how George's father in law had basically given him his entire election team from his time as Governor of Louisiana. Charles and William had been working in Washington at the time and had mobilized a small army to get George elected. Peter had said it sounded more like a coronation than an election and Charlotte agreed. Still, Charlotte did think it was cool to follow her own cousin on her legislative app.

"Well I was very impressed with Thunderbolt's benefit last year for the school system," Elizabeth said sitting forward and flashing a smile. "Ian and I were there and were quite impressed. Who did you use for the planning?"

"We took care of it in house," Peter said.

"Really?" Elizabeth said. "It was so well done, I figured you had hired someone."

"Thank you," Peter said. "We haven't done a lot of big event benefits like that, but a few of my employees were talking about the school their kids went to needing some structural upgrades so we all just pitched in and it turned out pretty well."

"Well I'd love to help you with your next event."

Peter sat back a bit, shuffling his hands a bit. "That's very nice, but we don't really do events. It was kind of a one-time thing."

"Speaking of a one-time thing, did you hear about the Hiller's son?" Uncle Mark said, steering the conversation back to gossip about people Charlotte didn't know. She settled back in her Adirondack chair and sipped her champaign, taking Peter's hand whenever he was able to sit back and relax. By the end of the third bottle, Uncle Matthew decided it was getting late and the rest of the older generation made their way up to the house. Peter looked after them and then back at Charlotte.

"I'm pretty beat too, you want to go in babe?"

"Oh you aren't ready to go in yet, are you Peter?" asked Charles.

"I'm kind of an early to bed, early to rise person," Peter half lied. Charlotte was definitely the early to bed, early to rise one. Peter was known to stay up all hours, working whenever the mood struck him. She actually really appreciated the excuse to head in earlier than she normally would have.

The newlyweds managed to escape after another twenty minutes and headed back inside. Charlotte grabbed her purse and laptop bag as she led Peter upstairs to the small loft bedroom she'd stayed in since childhood. When they got upstairs and into the room, Peter flopped down on the bed and let out a loud sigh. Charlotte shut the door and looked at her husband. His legs hung off the bed and he stretched out before folding his hands behind his head and staring at the ceiling. She'd always slept alone in this little room with the double bed that went almost wall to wall in the little space. It was almost strange seeing a man in her bed, even though that man had been in her bed for the last five months. She took her shoes off and gently climbed on the bed, straddling him and lowering herself softly on his thighs.

"You did great down there. I know there's a lot of them."

"It's not that." Peter said.

"Then what's wrong?"

Peter propped himself up slightly on his elbows and considered his next words.

"I feel like I just left a sales meeting."

"What do you mean?"

"I mean..." Peter readjusted himself and Charlotte sat next to him with their backs against the wall. "I don't have a big family. I don't have any Aunts and Uncles or cousins. So maybe I'm reading this all wrong, but I don't feel like they got to know Peter at all."

"What do you mean?" Charlotte asked, genuinely confused. "You were answering questions all night. Everyone was talking to you."

"Yeah but think about the conversation. Think about the questions. Elizabeth wants to organize my next corporate event. Charles wants to run an ad campaign for Thunderbolt on our PPE production when the pandemic started. William wants to talk about expansion into bigger markets. Everyone wants to know about my costuming deals and putting together a press blitz for award season. Everyone wants to know if I know this family or that family and if I've thought about working with these people or those people."

Charlotte nodded along as Peter recounted the evening's conversation.

"Well, you're interesting. You're new."

"But it wasn't me. It was all about P.J. Li."

"Forgive me, I'm only married to you so I might not understand, but aren't you and P.J. the same person?" Charlotte teased him slightly.

Peter laughed a little, then put his head back for a minute, trying to figure out what he wanted to say.

"Do you remember how mad you were at me when you first learned that I hadn't told you I owned Thunderbolt?"

"Little bit."

"You hit the nail on the head. Peter and P.J. are two different people. P.J. runs the business, but you married Peter. I was kind of hoping your family was interested in Peter before they were interested in P.J. That's one of the things I love about you. You love Peter and you tolerate P.J."

Charlotte leaned in and kissed Peter and then took his hand.

"I'm sure they are going to love getting to know Peter tomorrow."

Peter smiled at Charlotte and leaned in to her, kissing her deeply, before pulling her back to the mattress and being thankful for a quiet box spring.

2020
Saturday

Charlotte woke up to the sound of the woods for the first time in weeks. She had adjusted to the sounds of the city more easily than she thought she would, although her first night sleeping in New York had been a restless one. She had never really thought the outdoor noises at the cottage resembled the noises in Vermont, but after a few weeks of city living, she was amazed how the sound of birds and the gentle rustle of trees was actually pretty similar no matter where you were. Or maybe it was the other way around and she had just adjusted to city life better than she thought.

She looked over at Peter, laying on his stomach with his arms under the pillow, still asleep. She let her eyes follow his broad back to the blanket that lay just past his waist, and let her gaze stay on the curve of his ass for a few extra seconds.

God he's good looking.

Without waking him up, Charlotte slipped out of bed and got dressed, throwing a sports bra on under a comfortable short sundress and capri leggings. She opened and closed the door softly and went downstairs. As was common at the reunion, she was the first one up, so she made a pot of coffee and got an extra coffee pot out so there would be enough for everyone. She found she usually needed to brew three or four pots every morning to have enough, so she was glad she was such an early riser.

As soon as the first pot was done brewing, she emptied it into the serving container (minus a cup for herself) and started to brew pot number two. She took her coffee to the back porch and settled into a rocking chair and settled in with her phone to read the news.

The creak of the porch to the left of her grabbed her attention and she looked over to see her cousin Trevor's wife Taylor shifting her yoga pose. She hadn't even noticed her on the other side of the porch.

Taylor Rose had been acting professionally since she was sixteen. Charlotte had known who she was long before Trevor had married her. She'd done a few teen flicks that were right up the alley of her friends so Charlotte had gone to plenty of movies with her friends in middle and high school starring Taylor Rose. Lately, she'd moved into rom-coms and the latest news buzzing around the house was she was doing her first 'serious' film. Something period in England. She'd shown off her English accent last night around the campfire and talked about how the film was already getting Oscar buzz. How a film could generate Oscar buzz before it was even made was beyond Charlotte, but apparently it was an amazing script and going to be the break out role for Taylor to move into being taken seriously as an actor.

Again, how all this was possible before the film was even made, made absolutely no sense to Charlotte.

Frankly, she didn't understand why Taylor felt the need to be taken 'seriously' as an actress. She already had a more successful career than most people who tried acting. She had every advantage. Her father was a director or producer or something, and her mother was also an actress. Taylor herself was very good. Charlotte had liked the movies she'd seen and thought she was very good in the light hearted movies she did. She was also drop dead gorgeous. As she gracefully moved into another pose, Charlotte noticed she was almost impossibly thin. She honestly wondered how all her organs fit in there. Of course, she was also out on the deck doing yoga at 6am while on vacation and based on the running shoes and almost empty water container, Charlotte guessed she'd gone for a run prior to the yoga. Charlotte supposed these were the sacrifices one had to make to be an actress.

Honestly, Charlotte's extra ten or fifteen pounds were worth not putting herself through that sort of torture.

Taylor shifted position again and Charlotte came into her line of vision.

"Oh. Good morning Charlotte."

"Good morning Taylor. Sorry am I bothering you? I didn't even realize you were out here."

"Oh no its fine I'm done," she said as she grabbed her water and took a drink.

"Do you want some coffee?" Charlotte asked. "I just brewed a pot and started filling up the carafe.

"No, I don't really drink coffee," she said, taking another swig from her water bottle and stepping a little closer to Charlotte.

"So how is married life Charlotte?"

"The first four days have been pretty good. We'll see how day five goes," Charlotte joked as she took another sip of coffee.

"Must be a big adjustment for you though."

"Not really," Charlotte considered. "Peter and I clicked really fast and we started living together while he was in Vermont during the shutdown, so it really doesn't feel that much different."

"Still," Taylor said as she sat down next to her. "Different world than you're used to, right? I mean...he's P.J. Li. I have to admit, I was a little star struck when I heard who you'd married."

"Well, he's just Peter to me," Charlotte said.

"Well welcome to our world," Taylor said. "It's a fishbowl, but it has nice perks. And everyone gets to know everyone. For instance, did you know I actually met P.J. the first time I went to the Oscars?"

Charlotte knew how Peter went to award shows occasionally, if he'd designed something for an actress, or done some costume work on a movie that had been nominated, but she hadn't realized Taylor remembered him from an actual event.

"No I didn't realize that."

"Well I doubt he would remember me," Taylor said. "I was so star struck my first red carpet walk I could hardly function!" Taylor laughed a little. Charlotte nodded politely.

"Well anyway," Taylor continued "I'm a huge fan of Mei Tao, and she was presenting that year. My agent managed to introduce me, and this was back when she was dating P.J. so they were there together and I met them both. Isn't that funny?"

"Hilarious," Charlotte said flatly.

"Like I said, it's a fishbowl and all the fish know each other."

Charlotte saw an opening to lay some groundwork for Peter.

"Well I hope you get a chance to really get to know Peter this weekend. He's excited to get to know everyone. He doesn't have any cousins, so this is a new experience for him."

"I'm hoping to get to know him too. Maybe I can convince him to style me for next year's award season, huh? Now that we're family and all."

Charlotte sighed and covered it by blowing on her coffee. This was exactly what Peter didn't want, but she didn't know how to turn the conversation. Maybe she'd just have to run interference between Taylor and Peter the rest of the weekend.

As if on cue, the door opened and Peter appeared, cup of coffee in hand.

"Hey babe. I saw the carafe next to the coffee maker, so I dumped the pot into it and started another pot."

"Thank…" Charlotte started as Taylor stood up and flashed a smile.

"That was so nice of you!" Taylor said. "I was just going to grab a cup."

Charlotte furrowed her brow, confused by Taylor's sudden reversal on coffee drinking, but didn't have long to think about it as Trevor suddenly appeared on the porch, holding he and Taylor's one year old daughter Zara.

"See? There's mommy!" He said as the baby reached for her mother. Taylor took her with a smile and Charlotte was once again amazed by how thin

Taylor was and wondering how she had managed to have a baby.

Maybe there aren't any organs in there and it was just all baby.

Peter took the opportunity to sit in the chair next to Charlotte and looked up at Taylor and Trevor.

"She's beautiful."

"Oh thank you. She actually just did her very first national campaign last month." Taylor said towards Zara in a light, baby tone.

"Wow," exclaimed Peter in slight disbelief. "Following in the family footsteps early, huh?"

"Yeah, Uncle Luke and Uncle Mark were running a campaign for Pampers and hired Zara," Taylor said towards Peter before turning back to her daughter. "She did so good!" she said in her baby voice, prompting more laughter from Zara. Peter and Charlotte smiled and shot each other a glance. These were the sort of family moments Charlotte was hoping Peter would see, and she could see how pleased he was in that moment.

It didn't last.

"You know," Taylor's baby voice was gone as she looked at Peter, "Thunderbolt makes so many wonderful things, I'm shocked there's not a baby line."

Peter shifted uncomfortably in his chair.

"That's actually something that's in early development."

"Really!" Taylor stepped a little closer to Peter. "Oh it would be fantastic to do some collaborating on that. Zara and I could be your spokesmodels! How fun would that be?"

Peter shifted his shoulders and cleared his throat. *Interference time.*

"We should probably get going if we want to get that walk in before breakfast." Charlotte said quickly as she saw Taylor starting to gear up for a more lengthy conversation.

Peter looked at Charlotte with total confusion for a split second before he caught on.

"Right!" He looked back at Taylor and stood up. "Excuse us. We're still kind of on our honeymoon, so, we're going to take a little walk. Alone."

"Oh of course," Taylor said taking a step back. "Plenty of time to talk business later."

Peter smiled politely and took Charlotte's hand as the two of them took off toward the lake. He squeezed her hand and they looked at each other as Peter silently mouthed 'thank you' and Charlotte smiled.

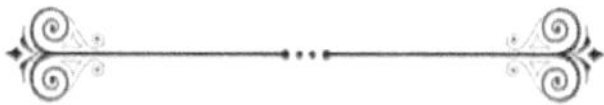

Charlotte and Peter returned to a bustling cottage and hour later. Most of the family had gotten up and was filling up plates and sipping coffee from the breakfast buffet Lindsey had set up in the time the newlyweds had been gone. They managed to sneak in the living room from the back porch and hide in the corner while Peter took in the small village he was now a part of.

"Ok, help me put faces with names," he quietly said to Charlotte. She started pointing to various family members, who, fortunately for Peter's sake, were grouped together by nuclear family more or less.

"Ok, let's do this in order." Charlotte started, directing Peter's eyes to the left.

"That's Uncle Matthew, Dad's oldest brother. He's married to Aunt Margaret…the one with the gaudy necklace."

Peter laughed slightly. "And they have one kid?"

"Two," Charlotte corrected. "It's easier if you just remember that all my Aunts and Uncles have two kids."

"Right. George and Elizabeth are their kids."

"There you go," Charlotte said. "George is married to Olivia, and they have two kids, Michael and Sarah. Elizabeth is married to Ian, and they have Catherine and Alice."

"Ok. So uncle Matthew's kids have the battle of the accents. Louisiana vs England with a little New York thrown in there."

Charlotte giggled. She'd never thought of how worldly that branch of the family had become.

"Next is Uncle Mark and Aunt Julia," Charlotte continued looking over at where they were sitting.

"They have the twin sons, right?" Peter asked.

"Right. Charles and William. Charles married Rebecca, William is with Bella, and they each have two kids. Robert and Rachel for Charles, Philip and Jacob for William."

Peter winced.

"I got that backwards yesterday and no one corrected me. Oops."

"It's a lot to remember. I'm sure you were forgiven."

Peter looked over to the far corner of the room.

"That's a California group, right?"

"Essentially," Charlotte confirmed. "Uncle Luke and Aunt Ana are still in New York, but I think they might move out to California to be near Trevor and Taylor now that they have Zara. And if they go, I'd be surprised if Travis doesn't go out there too with Koi."

"Where's Koi's mom?"

"Don't know. She and Travis were really into drugs I think, and Travis got clean, but Savannah didn't, so Travis has full custody. We really haven't seen Savannah in years."

"I'm sorry to hear that," Peter said with genuine concern.

"Travis has a good support system. Aunt Ana was a model back in the day, so she saw a lot of that stuff and got him into rehab. He's actually a really good dad and has come a long way since those days."

"Good for him," Peter said as he looked around and let his eyes stop on his father in law.

"And that one's you dad, right?" Peter joked.

"I think so. It's hard to tell through the crowd," Charlotte quipped back.

"Is there going to be a test on this?" Peter asked as he glanced at Charlotte and smiled.

"I'll give you another day to study."

"This is why I love you."

Charlotte laughed and looked up as her father finally noticed they had come in and wandered over.

"Well hello you two. Did you enjoy your walk?"

"Very much," Peter said. "Charlotte's told me all about this place but she really didn't do it justice. It's even prettier than she said."

"It's one of my favorite places on the planet," John said, looking back on his family before turning back to Peter and Charlotte. "The nannies are taking the children to the children's museum in town for the morning while we go out on the boat."

"The children's museum is open?" Charlotte asked, genuinely confused. Many places were still closed due to the pandemic, and a museum full of children all touching the same things seemed like a problem.

"Mom made a few calls and broke out the checkbook so it'll just be the Parker brood."

"Wow, that was generous of her," Charlotte said, surprised, but not really surprised. Grandma Evelyn was known for her ability to make things happen with just a few phone calls and a little help from her checkbook.

"And what do we do while the children are having the time of their lives at the museum?" Peter asked, half towards John, and half towards his wife.

"Grandma has a yacht out in the deep part of the lake. We swim, get sun, play games, and drink an obscene amount of alcohol."

"Sounds like a party."

Peter and Charlotte went over and got some breakfast, then stayed out of the fray of parents and nannies getting children ready to go, before getting themselves ready with swimsuits and enough sunscreen to cover an elephant. (Peter burned so badly his first trip out to California he joked he needed SPF 5,000) By 10:30, the children were happily playing at the museum and the adults were passing around mimosas on the boat deck. Peter stayed close to Charlotte while she ran interference, gently nudging the conversation away from Thunderbolt any time Peter took an uncomfortable drink or cleared his throat. After an hour or so, things seemed to calm down and everyone arranged themselves on the deck chairs or jumped overboard for a swim. Charlotte and Peter sat themselves on the swim board on the back of the boat, dangled their feet in the water, and started on their second mimosas.

"Thanks for driving the conversations." Peter said giving his wife a quick kiss on the forehead.

"You're welcome."

"I'm starting to wonder if they think I live at Thunderbolt."

Charlotte laughed a little.

"They probably do."

"Where's your cousin Elizabeth? It's not that big of a boat. I couldn't have missed her."

"She never comes out on the boat," Charlotte said taking another sip. "No wifi."

Peter laughed softly. "Is she really that addicted to Facebook?"

"No. She's probably working. She spends most of her day working while we're here. Sometimes she even heads back in to the city or she only stays for a day because she's working."

"She can't take a few days off?"

"She runs her own company. She's busy."

"I run my own company and I take a few days off here and there."

"True," Charlotte said. She had never really thought anything of her cousin's work ethic. Elizabeth had always been a very driven person, and ever since she started her company, she seemed to work around the clock. Charlotte remembered her taking a work call last year on Christmas.

"Isn't that what you used to do?" Charlotte asked Peter. "You said you used to work nonstop and that was basically your twenties, right?"

"I did," Peter said looking out over the lake. "I could probably have grown Thunderbolt bigger or done more costuming gigs, but I couldn't keep that pace up."

Charlotte laughed lightly.

"I guess she just hasn't grown out of her work around the clock phase."

He looked at Charlotte with that deep, penetrating look she'd fallen in love with just a few short months ago.

"Well I'm glad I outgrew it."

She leaned in and kissed her husband before a small splash of water grabbed the couple's attention. They looked down and saw George swimming a few feet away, his hands ready to splash them again.

"Alright lovebirds, break it up," He teased before turning his attention fully on Peter. "Come on in swimming and let Charlotte join in on the age old tradition of wives sitting in groups drinking and complaining about their husbands."

Peter smiled and looked back at Charlotte.

"Well it's been less than a week, so I'll probably get off pretty easy."

Peter stripped off his shirt and handed it to Charlotte before scooting himself into the lake and swimming out with his new cousins. Charlotte smiled and took another sip of her drink, finishing it and getting up to bring the glass back to the small kitchenette. She rinsed the glass out and glanced over at the boat deck. Laying out in the sun were her cousin's wives, Olivia, Rebecca, Bella, and Taylor. The four of them laughed and talked, sipping their drinks and sunning themselves. Charlotte wondered if they kept up the same exercise regime as Taylor, who was certainly the thinnest of the group, but not by much.

Charlotte went over and sat down on a lounge chair near them and Bella looked up at her.

"Hello Charlotte."

"Hi," Charlotte responded, readjusting herself on the chair.

"Charlotte, darling," Olivia started, "where ever did you find that...suit."

Charlotte looked down at her swim wear. The board shorts and tankini top which were in direct conflict with the tiny bikinis the rest of the group was wearing.

"Just at Target I think," Charlotte answered. There was a small chorus of 'Oh' from the women as they all fell quiet and fell into an awkward silence. Charlotte shifted and broke the silence.

"I was actually telling Peter how much I hate bathing suit shopping. I want something cute, but most of the cute bathing suits are super skimpy or don't look good on me, so I look for something with a little more coverage, but then its ugly, and so I end up with board shorts. I think he might look at starting a swimwear line at Thunderbolt."

The quartet perked up at the mention of a new line out of Thunderbolt.

"Well look at you influencing the world of fashion!" Taylor said.

"Maybe a new career path for you!" said Rebecca.

"Totally different than working in that musty bookstore, huh?" asked Bella.

"Library," corrected Charlotte. "I was the head librarian back home."

The quartet looked at her with furrowed brows for a beat before realization hit them. There was a chorus of 'Right!' 'Library! That's what I meant!' before the conversation turned back to jobs, kids, and who was doing what in the city. Charlotte sat and listened, not really understanding the references but figuring she should try to follow along now that she too was a New Yorker. It was particularly interesting how much Olivia knew, seeing as she had been born and raised in Louisiana, but Charlotte supposed after being married to George for a decade she must have gotten to know all 'the people'.

After what seems like three days of idle gossip about random people but was actually only 56 minutes (Charlotte had timed it) the quartet stopped in unison and looked at Charlotte. She awkwardly checked her top, glanced around her, and finally looked back at her cousins-in-law as she realized they were actually looking just past her to a glistening Peter who had just pulled himself out of the lake and was walking over to the ladies. Charlotte smiled as she looked back and forth between her husband and her cousins-in-law, enjoying the little bit of envy she didn't normally see from them as Peter joined her on her deck chair.

"So," Rebecca said to Peter, leaning forward slightly. "Charlotte tells us Thunderbolt is looking at starting a swimsuit line."

Peter shifted slightly.

"Yeah. Should be out in time for Spring Break," he said quickly.

"How exciting!" Bella chimed in.

"I always love it when Thunderbolt comes out with a new line." Taylor added.

"Thanks," Peter said before quickly turning his attention to Olivia. "How are the kids? Sarah's in kindergarten, right?"

"Yes she is." Olivia answered. Peter and Charlotte exchanged a quick glance and a smile, Peter relaxing slightly after successfully steering the conversation away from Thunderbolt.

It was short lived.

"She's already quite the little fashionista. She loves the computer bags you designed! I finally had to buy her one a few months ago. She carries it around all the time!"

Peter stiffened slightly. "That's cute."

"Just another reason to start that baby and children's line!" Taylor chimed in. "Zara and I are ready, willing, and able to be your official spokesmodels, so start designing!"

The quartet all started throwing out ideas about things that should be included in the hypothetical clothing line while Peter politely smiled and nodded. Charlotte tried to steer the conversation, bringing up the other children, the names of 'the people' they had been discussing earlier, projects at Parker Marketing...any other topic.

There was no steering.

All she could do was ride the rapids.

2020
Sunday

Charlotte shifted her position on the loveseat she was sharing with Peter, leaning in to him a little more. He glanced at her and quietly took her hand while they watched the sermon on the big TV over the fireplace. With church services still being remote around the country due to the pandemic, Charlotte couldn't spend time looking around the congregation at the familiar faces she saw every year. The only face she could watch was that of the pastor on the screen, and actually listen to his sermon, which had dragged on for twenty minutes so far.

She occasionally broke her gaze away and looked at her family, wondering if the other 'lake people' families were in their own lake houses, gathered around their own TVs watching the never-ending sermon, or if they skipped out when there were no other families to gossip with before and after the service.

Uncle Matthew and Aunt Julia sat on the couch with Grandma, Uncle Mark and Aunt Julia, all listening intently and nodding along. George, Olivia, Elizabeth and Ian took up space at the table behind them, sitting slightly more relaxed than the front row of Parkers but still at full attention...mostly. Charlotte caught Elizabeth checking her phone and sending a few texts or emails here and there. Uncle Luke had residence in the big armchair on the other side of the table, quietly checking his phone occasionally and glancing outside. Charlotte bet he needed a cigarette. Aunt Ana and Travis sat together nearby and Charles and William next to them with Rebecca and Bella. Charlotte wondered if Charles and Rebecca went to church or practiced Judaism at home.

Probably Judaism. Rebecca's more religious than Charles ever was.

She knew Bella was Jewish too, but she'd never really talked about it. She seemed engaged in the sermon, but you can be interested in a religion you don't practice, so maybe she was just intrigued by the endless droning.

Trevor and Taylor sat together in the oversized chair behind Charlotte, Peter, and her dad, so she couldn't see what they were doing, but she occasionally heard them comment on something, so maybe they were listening intently or maybe doing the same thing she was doing. She turned her attention back to the TV as she heard the pastor raise his voice slightly, hopeful he was reaching the end.

"And so my friends, I say to you...do as Luke wrote. Sell your possessions. Give to the needy. Then, and only then will you be rewarded with the true treasure of heaven."

Charlotte giggled silently to herself as the final hymn started playing and everyone started singing along in several dissonant keys. She tried to imagine someone actually selling everything they had to give to the poor. Granted, that would be an amazing show of kindness, but then, wouldn't the generous person just be poor? Then someone else sells everything they have and gives it to the first guy, the second guy is poor and a third guy seems everything he has and gives it to the second guy...

Kind of a weird, global game, but could be fun.

Charlotte looked around at her family again, wondering if any of them would ever sell all their possessions and give them to the poor. She looked at her father, who probably came the closest to doing that, but really, she knew he had tons of money stashed away in several accounts and investments and was still easily a millionaire even after leaving Parker Marketing. She looked at her Aunts and Uncles, who had all retired over the last few years, but still served on the board of directors, or had positions on other boards that paid them huge sums in addition to whatever retirement packages they had from Parker.

Are you actually retired if you still go into offices and get paid? Even if it's only a few times a month?

She looked at her cousins, the current leaders of Parker Marketing, a Congressman, and a power couple from Hollywood. She had grown up with these people, but she was suddenly very aware of how much of an outsider she was. There wasn't one person in the room that wasn't a millionaire. There wasn't one person in the room that went to public school. There wasn't one person in the room that cut coupons before heading to the grocery store.

Except her.

She chastised herself slightly. Peter had had a fairly normal childhood. He was a millionaire now, but he'd had very similar experiences to her growing up.

He's a millionaire now. Because he started a multi-million dollar company.

Charlotte felt her whole being sink. She'd always been happy with her life, proud of what she had done back home at the library. But suddenly, as her family stood around the TV in the living room singing How Great Thou Art, she felt about three inches tall. Everyone in her family was...important. Influential. They were famous and powerful, they did spots on TV and had articles written about them.

How long was it going to take Peter to realize he was a member of this club and she had no business being there?

She felt her throat close up slightly and she tried to slow her breathing down, but she couldn't stop her eyes from watering slightly as she tried harder and harder to stop it. This was ridiculous! She had grown up with these people. They had always been wealthy. Why was this suddenly bothering her so much?

The hymn ended and the final benediction given. Grandma exclaimed it to be an excellent sermon as Uncle Mark turned the TV off and Lindsey started setting out lunch. Everyone stared to head over to the table, grabbing plates and helping themselves to the sandwiches but Charlotte still felt like she couldn't breathe. She looked over at the table and saw Peter with her cousins, and she couldn't help but notice how natural he looked. He was very relaxed at home with her, but she thought about the man she had seen on the 22nd floor of that office building. The business man who made and spent millions of dollars a day. The man who flew out to California to oversee final costume designs for movies. The man who had back to back meetings and two assistants.

It was the first time she'd really seen him like that.

Her throat got even tighter. She couldn't breathe.

Charlotte headed out to the back porch and didn't stop until she was on the bank of the lake. She took a few deep breaths and paced back and forth, trying to calm herself down and get enough oxygen, but her eyes started watering, making her throat even tighter in a vicious cycle of panic.

"There you are." Peter said, smiling as he came to meet her on the shore. She turned to face him fully and his beautiful smile was gone in an instant, replaced with a look of panicked concern as he quickened his pace and hugged his wife, wrapping his arms around her as she melted into him and let the tears flow freely. Peter rocked gently and let his wife cry for a few minutes, letting her calm down before he spoke.

"What's wrong?"

"Everything," Charlotte said softly.

"I can see that," Peter said. "You want to narrow it down to the biggest issue?"

Charlotte broke away from him and wiped her face, resuming her pacing.

"It's so stupid," She started, laughing at herself through the tears.

"Tell me."

She looked at him, his arms crossed, and his face serious as he waited to hear his wife's troubles. She was suddenly embarrassed to share with him. She was embarrassed for how she felt. She was embarrassed for not keeping control of herself. She was supposed to be protecting and supporting him in this new adventure of meeting his new extended family. She was supposed to be making him feel welcome and at ease. She wasn't supposed to be the one feeling like an outsider.

Her breathing had finally returned to normal. Her brain was still racing, trying to figure out what to say. How to explain what was wrong. She couldn't wrap her head around her feelings fast enough, and the words just started spilling out.

"Everyone in that house is a multimillionaire. Everyone in that house is gorgeous, and successful, and I am just very aware of the fact that I am none of those things. I have never been any of those things and I never will be. And that was fine. It was fine. Because I lived in Vermont, and I had my own thing going on, and a few times a year, I would go to New York, see everyone, and go home to my life. But now? I live in their world. No matter how normal we try to be, we live in their world. I am just an unemployed invader who is going to go with you to events, and say the wrong thing, or have no idea what anyone is talking about, or wear the wrong thing, and I don't know how to deal with this. I don't know how to do this."

Peter's face relaxed as his wife's soul spilled all over the ground. He took a few steps to her and wrapped her up in his arms again, before stepping back with his hands on her arms.

"I started Thunderbolt when I was 20 in my dorm room. I remember having meetings with investors that all had custom tailored suits and corner offices and I was just this dumb college kid who was asking them for money. The first costume design deal I got was for a small, independent film in New York, and they took me to this really fancy place for lunch, and I needed to wear a suit coat. I didn't own one at the time. I borrowed one from Tom, and considering how much taller Tom is than me, you can imagine how good that looked."

Charlotte laughed at the image of Peter's five foot ten inch frame drowning in a suit coat made for the six foot five inch 250 pound frame that Tom sported.

Peter laughed with her.

"I think I was just too young and stupid at the time to really realize how out of place I was. I built Thunderbolt up for years. I learned how to navigate this insane world over years. We've been together for 7 months. We've been married for less than 7 days. You can't expect yourself to adjust to things that fast."

"I've had 29 years of experience being in this family Peter. I shouldn't have to adjust."

"But you said it yourself. You've always been a visitor. You had your life in Vermont and you occasionally visited these people."

Charlotte's breathing started to slow down.

"I just hate the fact that I feel like this with my own family."

"Honestly, Charlotte," Peter paused, choosing his words.

"If these people weren't your family, would you want to be with them? The only thing I've seen from them all weekend is a blatant disregard for you. I've seen you make excuses for them, and give them love, and they basically ignore you."

Charlotte sighed.

"They just have a lot going on and I don't really..."

"Stop making excuses for them!" Peter gently cut his wife off. The pair looked at each other for a few beats while Peter lightly stroked his wife's arms.

"If the best you can be for them is a visitor, then that's what it is. Don't let that define you."

He smiled at her and let his hands slide down her arms to her hands.

"And who the hell cares if you aren't a multimillionaire? Who decided that is what makes you successful?"

"Basically all of human civilization," Charlotte quipped.

"Point," Peter laughed lightly with his wife. "But honestly, you are successful. You are at the beginning of a new journey right now, and I'm going to be right there with you and you are going to define success however you want to define it."

Charlotte smiled weakly and squeezed her husband's hands. How had she gotten this lucky? She wouldn't have been surprised at all if he had just walked the other way while she fell to pieces. But here he was...supporting her through the small bout of insanity.

"Let's go back in and have some lunch," Peter suggested. "We can sit in the corner and be outsiders together."

Chapter 9

Wednesday, September 1, 2021

Charlotte flushed the toilet and sat back on the floor, quickly giving up on a seated position and laying down flat on her back. She grabbed the washcloth off the bathtub and put it back on her forehead, grateful for the water dripping down her temples but wishing it was cooler. She took a few deep breaths and enjoyed the quiet for a minute before the silence was broken by Peter's footsteps across the bedroom to the bathroom door.

"We're not going."

Charlotte opened her eyes slightly and watched Peter as he brought himself down to the floor and sat in the bathroom doorway.

"We need to go," Charlotte groaned out. "It's important to my dad."

"It's important to your dad that you spend the entire weekend puking at the cottage instead of puking here at home?"

"You know what I mean."

Peter took the washcloth off Charlotte's head, brushed some hair back off her forehead, and stood up to rewet it.

"I know you don't want to let your dad down, but he will understand."

Peter wrung the washcloth out, refolded it, and rejoined his wife on the floor. The fresh cool washcloth felt like heaven.

"If you want to go to the cottage on Friday, we'll go. But you'll just be miserable the entire time."

"I can puke at the cottage just as easily as I puke here," Charlotte tiredly quipped.

"I'm not talking about the morning sickness and you know it."

Charlotte groaned.

"Morning sickness. What a stupid name. More like 'whenever it damn well feels like it' sickness."

Peter smiled and took Charlotte's hand. She looked up at him and smiled. Peter had been an absolute godsend the past few months. Her doctoral program had gotten particularly difficult when she was assigned to a new professor who made her basically throw out everything she had been working on and start from scratch. Then, Grandma Evelyn had died in July. Charlotte had spent the three weeks before she died visiting, and even though she'd always been close to her Grandmother, they'd really gotten close at the end. Then, four weeks later, Charlotte had gotten sick and a pregnancy test had confirmed why. They were thrilled, but it had been quite a roller coaster of a summer.

Now, he looked at her with that concerned looked she'd gotten used to. He tried to hide it, but she could tell he was worried about her.

"I will never stop you from seeing your family." Peter started, "But I want you to honestly think about why you want to go. What exactly are you looking forward to? Besides your Dad, who exactly are you looking forward to seeing?"

"They're my family Peter."

"Yes and like I said, you want to go, we go."

Peter collected himself a little, stroking her hair lightly. He noticed how upset Charlotte was getting and quickly switched to his more logical argument.

"Let's also consider the fact that you have a mountain of research to do, all your stuff is here, and let's face it, you have a grape sized problem at the moment and it's calling the shots."

Charlotte smiled weakly, but genuinely, admitting defeat.

"You're right, you're right. We'll skip the reunion."

"Ok," Peter said, satisfied that his wife would be happy with the decision in the long run. He got up off the floor, straightened himself out, and looked back down at Charlotte. "Do you need anything before I go to work? Do you need any more books from the library?"

"Oh I hate to ask Greg to pick up more books for me," Charlotte said. Peter's assistant Greg had taken on the job of picking up books for Charlotte at the NYU library. It was certainly convenient, but Charlotte didn't like using Peter's employees as her personal assistants.

"Honestly Charlotte, its fine," Peter reassured her. "His girlfriend is a student so he enjoys the excuse to grab lunch and a quickie on campus."

Charlotte laughed and directed Peter to the list she had on her desk of the next round of books she wanted. He picked up the list, a box from his own desk, came back into the bathroom, and got down on his knees to kiss her good bye.

"Also, before I forget…" he put the box next to her on the floor.

"Happy Anniversary."

By lunchtime, Charlotte had managed to keep some crackers down and get a fair amount of work done when her phone rang. She smiled, seeing the beautiful amethyst ring Peter had gotten her for their first anniversary shining on her finger as she reached for her phone and answered brightly.

"Hey dad."

"Hi Charlie, how you feeling?"

"Better. This morning was rough but I'm alright."

"Your mom had the same problem," Her father said, his voice dripping with nostalgia. Charlotte smiled, picturing the look on her father's face. She and Peter hadn't planned on telling anyone about the pregnancy for a few weeks, but after they had had to cancel a few dinners with her father and Peter's mother due to Charlotte's inability to hold much of anything down, they ran out of excuses and told the expectant grandparents the good news.

"Well I'm amazed anyone has more than one kid if they have to go through this every time," Charlotte said, half joking.

Her father laughed. "It gets easier Charlie, I promise."

"I hope so," Charlotte said. "Peter and I are going to skip the reunion this year though. I'm just so miserable, I wouldn't have any fun and I really just need to stay home. I hope you aren't too upset."

"Not at all sweetie. It makes sense."

Charlotte silently sighed in relief.

"Thanks Dad."

"Well anyway," her father changed topics. "I needed to call you because I have some interesting news for you."

"Ooo, how intriguing. Do tell."

"Well, you know that I'm in charge of mom's estate."

"Yes," Charlotte said. Her grandmother had been very smart and set everything up in her last few years and had asked her lawyer son John to take care of all the legal aspects of her death. It had amazed Charlotte exactly how much time and effort it took to legally die in America. Especially when there was a lot of money and property involved. Her father had said he thought he would be working on this for the next year.

She needed to remind her father he was not allowed to die. She didn't want to deal with a year of legal paperwork. And not being a lawyer, she imagined it would take her significantly longer.

"Well in dealing with mom's will, I've started dividing things up according to her wishes. There's some jewelry coming your way, and a few of the paintings from her place, but there's one piece in particular I thought you'd be very interested in."

"What's that?"

"The Cottage."

Charlotte almost dropped the phone. She hadn't expected to get anything from her Grandmother's will, assuming things would be divided between her four children. She knew her Grandmother had a massive jewelry collection and kind of thought she would get a few pieces, but other than that, she hadn't expected anything big. Most certainly not the Cottage.

"I'm sorry, the what?"

"The Cottage Charlie. Mom left it to you. She wanted you to run it like a rental so it makes some money but keep it in the family so we always have a place to vacation and be together. She wrote you a letter about it, and I've got everything set for you to start renting it. You'll just have to figure out a system that works best for you for managing it. Several of the houses in the area operate as rentals, so I'm sure you can get ahold of one of the other families and see how they run the rentals and then come up with a system that works for you. Mom left a pretty good sized account for you to fund tax payments and upkeep, and moving forward, I think if you can rent it for ten or fifteen weeks out of the year you'll have plenty of money for upkeep and improvements for years."

Charlotte was shocked and didn't know what to say. She did love the property, and always wanted to spend more time there, and now it was hers. She wouldn't charge the family to use it of course, and she could still host reunions, and maybe they could do family Christmas out there, since they wouldn't have Grandma's big brownstone any more. And it could be kind of fun to run it as a rental. She could put together little welcome baskets for the guests and have a guest book and read about where everyone had come from.

"Thanks Dad. I'll get to work on this right away." Charlotte furrowed her brow and asked, "But one question...why me?"

"What do you mean Charlie?"

"Why me? Why did Grandma leave the Cottage and rentals to me? Wouldn't it have made more sense for you or one of your brothers, or really anyone who works at the company to do it? I don't have any business experience."

"Your Grandmother was a big believer in family first Charlie. She always loved bringing everyone together at the Cottage and that's the priority for her. She wants the place to make enough money to support itself, but she doesn't want it to leave the family, and she felt you would be the most fair minded person to run it that way."

Charlotte felt tears well up in her eyes. She had no idea her Grandmother had been planning to do anything like this. It was such a wonderful way for Charlotte to remember her grandmother.

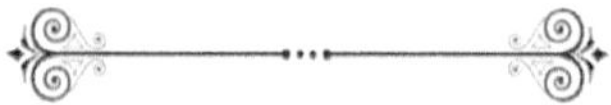

Charlotte took a welcome break from her work to take the Halloween decorations down off the apartment door and put up the Thanksgiving decorations. It had taken two months, but Charlotte was starting to feel like her old self again, finally getting up the energy to work and spending substantially less time on the bathroom floor. She finally felt like she was getting a handle on her research and dissertation, the baby's room was coming along nicely, and she had just accepted a job teaching an accelerated history course online for January and February.

She was also very grateful for yoga pants and the ability to do all these things from home so she could wear them. The last time she had tried to put on real pants had been depressing so she vowed not to make that mistake again.

Her phone started ringing. She sighed but quickly chastised herself. Her friends from Vermont had been calling her all morning to wish her a happy birthday. It was hard to be upset about people caring about you, so Charlotte waddled her way back to the dining room table and was shocked to see Charles on her caller ID.

"Hi Charles," Charlotte answered the phone cheerfully. She couldn't think of the last time her cousin had called her. This may have been the first time actually.

"Hi Charlotte. How are you?"

"I'm great. How are you?"

"I'm well, thanks," he said in a very business-like manner. "I wanted to talk to you about the Cottage."

"Yeah, I was actually going to put it out there about Thanksgiving," Charlotte said. "I thought it would be cool to have Thanksgiving out there since we don't have Grandma's house anymore."

"That's an idea," Charles said. "But I was actually looking beyond that. I wanted to talk about the property management."

"Oh yeah," Charlotte said. She had actually been working fairly hard on that over the last two months and was excited to share her progress with someone. She was planning on putting everything out to everyone in the next few weeks, but she was excited to give Charles a preview.

"You remember Benny, right? He used to work for Grandma and Grandpa. Well, he actually moved up near the Cottage a few years ago when he got married, and he started doing some property management in the area with some of the other houses up there. He actually has everything online and he said he'd be happy to manage our place too. I was relieved to have someone we know, you know? I know how much Grandma and Grandpa liked Benny, so it feels really good to have him involved in the Cottage."

"So can you pump the brakes on that?" Charles asked.

Charlotte furrowed her brow.

"What do you mean?"

"We were talking about the Cottage a few weeks ago at the office, and we think there are some different avenues we should go."

"Who's we?" Charlotte asked.

"At the office. We were just discussing the best course of action for the place. Obviously we all have a wealth of experience, we all dabble in real estate as well as being marketing experts, so we think we've come up with a comprehensive plan moving forward."

Charlotte was dumbfounded. What was Charles talking about? Why were her cousins having meetings about the Cottage without her? Granted, it was probably easy for them all to get together since they all worked in the same office building, but why hadn't any of them called her before? She lived in the city now. There was no reason she couldn't hop on the subway and be at Parker Marketing for lunch or a few meetings.

Maybe she was overthinking it. After all, her father had probably told everyone about the Cottage at the reunion, and since Charlotte hadn't been there, she wasn't able to tell everyone she was looking forward to managing the property.

"That's nice Charles, but honestly, I think I've got it under control."

"I'm sure you do," Charles cut her off, still using his most businesslike voice. "but we just feel we're better equipped to roll the property into our real estate holdings and handle the marketing in house."

Charlotte took a breath. She didn't like the way this conversation was going. She was a thirty year old woman working on a PhD. She wasn't a child. She wasn't incapable of what her Grandmother had instructed her to do. Granted, it was her first foray into real estate and property management, but she had educated herself and felt she could handle it.

Of course, most of her cousins thought she worked as a cashier at a bookstore, even after she reminded them several times she was currently a doctoral candidate. And even if she was a cashier at a bookstore, what about that would disqualify her from running a rental house?

Apparently in the Parker family, you are only capable of basic human functions if you work at a billion dollar company with your family name slapped on the top five stories of the building.

She could fix this.

"Here's an idea Charles," Charlotte started, using her best diplomatic tone. "If everyone wants to be involved in the decision making, it would make sense for us to all be in the same room. I was thinking about having everyone out to the Cottage for Thanksgiving. We can discuss everything then. I'll let everyone know about Thanksgiving, and we can go from there."

There was a slight pause on the other end of the phone, followed by Charles agreeing to talk about the issue later. Charlotte put her phone down, and quickly jotted 'Cottage Management Proposal' on her to do list.

Hopefully this dissertation would go smoothly the first time.

Charlotte threw the remnants of the turkey juice covered stick of butter away and waddled back to the sink to wash her hands. Peter took another sip of his coffee and then put the turkey in the oven before stepping over to the sink, running his fingers down Charlotte's back gently and giving her a quick kiss on the head.

They had come up to the cottage the night before in order to set up the house for the family Thanksgiving. Peter's mother was coming, as well as the entire Parker tribe. Charlotte had texted and left messages with her entire family to come out to the cottage and was quite excited about starting the new Thanksgiving tradition. Obviously, not having the day at her Grandmother's was going to be a little bittersweet, but hopefully, the change of venue would make everyone happy in spite of the matriarchal loss.

Charlotte sat down on the couch and cuddled up next to Peter to watch a movie. She went over her mental checklist...turkey was in the oven, mashed potatoes were in the crock pot, the other veggies were waiting by their assigned bowls and cooking dishes, pies were done, dishes were ready to be set out...she let herself relax and enjoy some down time before everyone arrived.

By noon, the second movie was ending and Peter and Charlotte were both in the kitchen, chopping, cooking, and setting the table. Peter's mom and Charlotte's dad arrived at 12:30, and by 1:00, everything was ready to serve.

By 1:10, Charlotte had made her way to the front door, watching for any arrivals.

By 1:20, Peter was pouring a second glass of wine for himself, his mom, and his father in law.

"You both knew we were starting at one, right?"

"Of course Charlie," her father answered. "That's why we got here at 12:30."

He took his phone out of his jacket pocket and got up from the couch.

"Let me call my brothers and see where everyone is. I'm sure they will show up as soon as I start calling."

Charlotte took another sip of her water and sat down at the table, straightening the silverware in front of her as Peter sat next to her.

"Everyone said they were coming, right?"

"I texted everyone and got thumbs up emojis. It's not exactly an RSVP but I thought..."

She trailed off and looked at her husband, a cold realization coming to her in a wave. She could feel her throat tighten and her eyes well up.

Rational Charlotte took over, calming irrational Charlotte down and relaxing her ever tightening throat.

No...they would have told me if they weren't coming.

She smiled a little and looked at Peter.

"I'm being ridiculous aren't I? They are just running late. Or maybe I told them two. Pregnancy brain," she said with a wave of her hand

Peter put his glass down and leaned in to his wife.

"You said one Charlotte."

"Peter, I must have had the time wrong. We always have Thanksgiving together, so everyone knows to be here. I'm sure I just messed up the time."

Peter took her hand.

"Charlotte, you don't make mistakes like that."

Charlotte looked at Peter and felt her throat starting to tighten up again as her father walked over while putting his phone back in his jacket pocket.

"So I just spoke to Matthew. He and Margaret are at George and Olivia's. Apparently George decided to host and figured his apartment was the right size for his family, Elizabeth's family, and their parents. Mark and Julia did the same but just had their kids and grandkids over, and Luke and Ana's branch is out in LA at Trevor and Taylor's place. Matthew thought Mark had told you, Mark thought William or Charles had told you and so on and so on."

Charlotte felt herself tense up. She stared blankly ahead. They all texted her back. They had all sent different versions of 'ok' or a thumbs up. If they hadn't wanted to come, why didn't they just say that? Why make her think they were coming if they had decided to go elsewhere?

She needed air.

Charlotte pushed herself up off the chair and shuffled toward the back door. The crisp autumn air hit her face as she opened the door, bringing a welcome relief to the quiet sounds of silverware and plates being collected by her father, mother in law and husband as they took a meal set for almost thirty down to a meal set for four.

She took a few long breaths, looking out over the lake. The light from the afternoon sun reflecting off the still water calmed her down, but also reminded her how alone she was in that moment.

She heard the door open behind her, and Peter joined her on the porch. She always felt better when he was close, but the empty, lonely feeling remained. They stood in silence for a while…ten minutes…ten seconds…she couldn't tell. She could feel Peter occasionally looking at her, waiting for her to start. She had so many thoughts swirling around, but none of them stayed at the surface long enough for her to articulate.

"Why don't they like me?"

She didn't even think about it. The words had just come out of her. She hadn't even realized she'd said them at first, but then realized that the words were still hanging in the air, choking her. She could hear Peter take a deep breath and shift himself on the porch. Another silence descended on them…ten more minutes? Thirty seconds?

"It's not a matter of liking you," Peter started. "They're your family and they love you."

"Then why aren't they here?" she snapped, her gaze finally shifting towards her husband. "They could've told me they didn't want to do the big Thanksgiving like we did with Grandma and Grandpa. They could've said they wanted to stay with their nuclear family...stop doing the big get together. I would've understood. But they didn't even tell me. They all acknowledged the plans for the day and made me think they were coming, and then they didn't come."

She wiped the tears that had finally come. Peter stepped toward her and she clung to him, letting him stroke her back and try not to show how awkward he had to stand to accommodate her pregnant belly. She let herself release all the pent up frustration she had, feeling both better and worse at the same time.

Finally, the tears stopped, and she was just breathing, her head on Peter's shoulder, his hands still stroking her back slowly. She didn't want it to stop, and Peter probably would have gone on as long as she needed it, but she suddenly became aware of how awkwardly he was standing in order to hold her, so she took a deep breath and lifted herself off him.

"You have every right to be upset," Peter started softly. "And I know it feels like they don't love you, since this isn't how you deserve to be treated. You don't deserve to be treated like this by anyone, especially not your own family. And I do think they love you, insomuch as they are your family. But as for liking or disliking you...it's neither of those. They nothing you."

"What?"

"They nothing you," Peter said matter of factly, but with an undertone of deep caring.

"What does that mean?"

"Liking or disliking implies some strong feelings. I don't think they think about you enough to like or dislike you. You exist, they know you are related to them, but they don't have enough invested in you to actually worry about how you feel about anything. They nothing you."

Charlotte absorbed the words, trying to fully comprehend what had just been said. Her whole life, she'd been taught the importance of family. Her father had always said family first...family means everything...she believed that. She always had. It was a core value she thought everyone had. The Parker clan had always looked out for each other. They were all involved in everyone's lives, they all worked together...

But not me.

She let that thought resonate for a minute. She was so embarrassed that she hadn't seen it. She had just assumed the feelings were the same in every part of her family, but why would they be? Peter saw it. He saw it seven days into their marriage, but he still went to Parker Family Christmas and smiled and laughed...he and William even got to be pretty good friends for a little while before William took over a new division at Parker Marketing. He saw it. Why hadn't she.

Because she hadn't wanted to see it.

Charlotte looked back at Peter, her family that chose her. She took his hand and gave it a gentle squeeze.

"Let's go eat."

2025

I obviously don't remember this reunion. There's proof I was there, in pictures on my parents' phones and in the albums my mom put together throughout the years at the cottage. This particular year had produced one of my dad's favorite family pictures, so I saw it every time I was at his office, and he would bring it with him anytime he traveled. It was a picture of the four of us at the cottage, by the big staircase. My dad, happily holding four year old me in my little green baseball cap with 'Andy' embroidered on it. My mom, holding a copy of her first book in one hand and with the other, supporting my two year old sister who was sitting on the banister in a t shirt with a jar of jelly on it. Most of the pictures of my sister from when she was little had jelly on it, which was from her nickname.

Gwen Evelyn Li.

GELi.

I remember pointing out to my mom that 'G' didn't make a 'J' sound when I was learning how to read, but she explained to me that nicknames didn't always have to make sense. Of course, when one of my friend's moms had asked if they ever called me (Andrew James) A.J., my parents both shut that down fast, so I assumed nicknames really didn't make sense.

We went to the cottage every summer for a week with my Aunts and Uncles. Of course, my parents are both only children, so none of them were my actual relatives, but after growing up with my parent's friends...Janice, Katie, Hannah, Tom...they were essentially all Aunts and Uncles, so it make sense that I referred to them all as such. We would swim in the lake and play games, have campfires every night and play hide and seek throughout the big house.

Over Labor Day weekend, we would go back. My grandma and grandpa would come, and mom always said before we went that maybe my cousins would come this year, but it always ended up being just the six of us. I saw my cousins occasionally growing up. Sometimes at a playground we would run into them, and we went to Disneyland with our cousin Zara when we went with my dad to California on a month long business trip. Years later, my mom had our cousin Michael in one of the classes she taught at NYU. That was the extent of the interactions.

My mom always looked a little sad when she talked about how little we saw our cousins, but she would say that family is what you choose for it to be. No matter what, your family is still your family, but people grow apart. Families grow and change. It's just part of life. And while you don't shut the door, you have to accept that people may not want to walk through the door. So, the best thing to do is fill your life with people who are excited to see your open door and celebrate the relationships we choose to nurture.

About the Author

Elizabeth Darin grew up in a small town in Illinois and is now a music teacher, and part time writer. She lives in Illinois with her husband Andy, their kids, Tony and Naomi, and two cats.

www.ingramcontent.com/pod-product-compliance
Lightning Source LLC
Chambersburg PA
CBHW021156110726
47900CB00002B/591